Dreams of the Moon Bear

Rick Mallery

Email: mallery.rick@gmail.com

For Olga Orlova

Part I

Chapter 1

The man had enough. He wanted to get away. He went into his closet one night and decided to stay there until the next morning.

The man opened his closet door. He removed his laundry basket and almost everything else that cluttered the floor.

"People would think I'm crazy if they knew what I am doing," he told himself.

"But you are crazy," himself told him. "People don't see it because you have learned to hide it well."

"Thank you," he said.

"You are welcome," himself said.

The man spread a blanket on the floor of the closet. The closet was just the right size for him to lie down fully.

"It is dark too early these winter days," he told himself.

"It will be darker in the closet," himself said.

"That's why I am going in there."

The man took off his clothes and threw them on the bed. He looked at himself in the mirror.

"Twenty pounds would be enough. It shouldn't be too hard to lose twenty pounds," he told himself.

"You have lost it before and gained it all back. This is the weight that your lifestyle dictates," himself told him.

"There's honor in trying," he said.

"You don't believe in honor. There might be meaning in trying, but there's no honor."

"Meaning is enough."

"Then there is also meaning in gaining it back."

The man lay down on the floor of his closet. He had forgotten his pillow. He left the closet and took the pillow from his bed. He returned to the closet.

"Are you sure you want to do this?" himself asked him.

"I can be as crazy as I want to be when I am alone. It's an exercise of freedom."

"How is locking yourself in a small closet an exercise in freedom?"

"As long as a man is free to do unusual things—and as long as he occasionally does those unusual things—he is free."

"Who gains by this exercise if you do it in private?"

"I do. I am sure I will be a different man in the morning when I step out of the closet. Different than I have been to this point—different even than I am right now."

"You have not shut the door yet."

"I want this feeling of anticipation to linger."

"Are you sure you will go through with it?"

"Yes. I'm just reflecting on what has been. I am saying goodbye. Everything will be different, even you."

The man grabbed the bottom of the closet door and pulled it shut.

"What time will you let us out of here?"

"When the alarm clock rings—at the usual time."

"Then what will we do?"

"Then I will go to work as usual."

"So you expect things to be different even though you plan to do everything as usual?"

"Yes."

The man arranged himself on the blanket. He folded the blanket over on itself and lay between the two halves. The pillow lay on a few towels that he had not removed from the floor.

"The twenty pounds is hard to lose," he told himself, "because my weight is average for our society. I'm abnormal enough as it is without drawing attention to myself by being a healthy weight."

Himself did not answer him.

"But I would like to lose it someday."

Himself still did not answer him.

The man enjoyed the silence. He felt the madness of silence swirl through his mind, but he knew silence was what he needed most.

"Then why don't you just think silently to yourself instead of conversing with me out loud?" himself said.

"Because speaking out loud uses a different part of the brain than silent thought. It requires physical action. The tongue, the jaw, the teeth, and vocal chords. Listening to myself stimulates my ears, and I can feel the vibrations through my bones."

"People really would think you are crazy if they heard you talking out loud to yourself."

"As you said before, I *am* crazy. Although it is probably more accurate to say I am abnormal rather than crazy or insane. Those terms are ambiguous and lean toward rhetoric. I know I am not psychotic. I am able to keep my abnormalities to myself."

"For the most part."

"I don't need people to think I'm entirely normal either. It is enough to give them the hint that something odd might be going on in my mind—if they bothered to look close enough."

"And they don't bother to look close enough."

"No, they don't."

The man raised his arms, and his hands brushed against the bottom of his shirts.

"What are you doing?"

"Just getting the lay of the land."

The man turned on to his side and pulled up his knees. It had been his normal sleeping position ever since he was in the womb.

"Do you think it is fair for you to sleep so early?"

"I usually take a nap after work. Why not do it now? It's part of my routine."

The man put his arm under his pillow. He teased his hair with his hand.

"That tickles."

"I know."

The man fell asleep.

"Hey are you asleep?" himself asked him. "What am I supposed to do if I cannot sleep?"

He made no reply.

* * *

She was a woman long before she was a man sleeping in a closet. She was still a man sleeping in the closet, but she was also a woman walking on the moon. She was a woman walking on the moon, and she was alone.

She had wanted to get away, and she had gotten away by going to the moon where she could be alone.

The moon dust irritated her feet. It gathered in her shoe, and her heel rubbed against the gritty heel of her shoe, and it irritated her.

It irritated her, but not as much as being around people irritated her.

As a man, she had mastered not only being alone in a closet, but also having an intelligent conversation with himself. As a woman on the moon, she was content to think to herself and feel the emotions that the freedom of an empty planet and one-sixth gravity afforded.

The woman removed her shoes and walked barefoot across the moon dust. She stopped and wiggled her feet and they sunk deep into the gray powder.

She knew she was not crazy. She knew it with the same degree of certainty that her male alter ego knew he was crazy—or abnormal. She was not crazy. She was simply a bitch. The woman was uncertain whether she had been exiled to the moon or had retreated to the moon. In either case, it was the best for all concerned.

The man could represent their being well enough on earth, and he had the kind of psyche that could persevere in a hostile or poisonous environment without going totally insane. He simply had to retreat to the womb for a few hours and he was nearly as good as new.

The woman needed—no, demanded—the entirety of the universe in which to unleash her soul. And even the universe was not large enough.

She tried to think when it had happened—the rupture, that is. She could not remember what things had been like before the moon. She simply felt what the man experienced, and she had an intuition of their past life together through the tenuous connection they still shared. He did not think about her. He did not remember or intuit anything about her. He was unaware of her existence altogether. That should give you some idea about how they arrived at their present condition.

The sun rose over the horizon.

The woman lived on what the earthlings call the dark side of the moon. In fact, it was no darker than the earth's side of the moon. The far side of the moon is a more accurate description. The benefit of being on that side was that it had no view of earth, and just as important, the earth had no view of it.

When the earth saw the new moon, the far side was bathed in light. When the earth saw the full moon, the far side was sunless.

The woman could manage during the darkness. She could manage the cold, and she could manage the loneliness. She called it her aloneness, though: she never felt lonely. She had enough of a connection to the stinking, fat, lazy, stupid, ugly members of the human race through the man. That connection existed no matter the position of the sun or the relative position of the earth.

The woman was nude. She liked her shoes even though the moon dust irritated her feet when she wore them. But she did not like to wear anything else.

She was a bitch, so she seldom had erotic feelings. Her nakedness was not an erotic expression but an expression of freedom. The man made up for her portion of eroticism. She called him the slut. It might have been around the time that she had first called him a slut that she had found herself on the moon, but she doubted the man had had enough power to cast her off.

Once a year she could touch herself and make herself quiver all over for ten seconds. She blamed the man for that. In any case, it was a small enough compromise that she could suffer it well enough.

She was enough of a bitch that she did not even pay attention to the quality of her attractiveness. She could look at her breasts as simply two useless pounds of fat. She did not even notice that on the moon they only sagged one-sixth as much as they had on earth.

Nor did she pay any special attention between her legs. She shaved her pubic hairs—not from any erotic impulse, but simply to remove the irritation of the damnable hair.

She stood in the moon dust, which by now rose above her ankle.

Another human being approached her from the distance.

Her hackles raised, the woman found a boulder nearby and hid behind it.

The woman emptied her handbag and took an inventory of her weapons.

The nail file was inadequate; the revolver was useless. She could not explain how she could breathe on the moon but a pistol cartridge could not fire, nor did she feel the need to. The hair band she could use to tie wrists together, and the tissue paper she could use to daub away tears before strangling the stranger with the cord of her curling iron.

She would make do with something. She was not an adaptive mammal for nothing.

The shadow of the intruder fell across the boulder signaling that the moment of action was at hand.

* * *

The tree stood near the rocky beach of a cold island in the North Pacific Ocean. Its grand hope was that it was on Sakhalin Island, but as far as it knew, it could be on one of the Aleutian Islands. It did not know very far because it was a tree, and a tree does not know very much because it has a tiny brain.

Popular wisdom holds that plant life does not have a nervous system, but tell that to a tall fir on the shore of a cold island in the North Pacific when a grizzly bear passes by.

Indeed this tree had enough of a brain to be afraid of grizzly bears. It also had enough of a brain to harbor hope that its existence persisted on Sakhalin Island rather than one of the Aleutians.

Fear and hope. If the tree had had a little bigger brain than it did have, it would have replied that its fear of bears and its hope to exist in one place rather than another were irrational processes. And everyone with a large enough brain knows that the brain is only responsible for the rational thought processes. The irrational processes in living beings are the products of the circulatory system. And while a tree does not need a heart to pump blood throughout the body as animals do, it has an efficient capillary system that effectively circulates water from the roots to the tips of the branches—and everywhere in between—in addition to producing the sap that humans find so useful.

A tree could have written Einstein's paper on capillary action eons before Einstein existed—if a tree had a large enough brain to write at all.

But as a tree has a very small brain, this tree did not know that its fear of bears and its hope that it lived on Sakhalin Island emanated from its veins rather than its brains.

But that is the universal nature of all idiots: they always feel that they know more than they do. If this means that all living things are idiots, than who am I to argue? And the tree would argue even less—having a smaller brain than I do. As far as that goes, who is to say that even inanimate objects do not share in universal idiocy too? The rock near the tree might have just enough brain to fear the tree, as all fir trees are sure that all things in existence are afraid of fir trees. Even grizzly bears. Had not the tree's mother always told it that the bears are even more afraid of it than it is of them?

But this tree had only seen one bear. And oh, if only the tree could claw back at the bear in the way that the bear clawed at the tree! Yet, when the tree was honest, it would have to admit that it did get aroused by such abuse. But the tree was too shy to be honest about such things. Or perhaps the tree was not intelligent enough to be honest about such things.

The way the long claws embedded themselves deep in the flesh of the tree and released it from the suffocating pressure of the bark that had grown too tight was highly erotic to a tree at that age.

If the tree had a larger brain and better communication skills, it would have equated this pleasurable pain to a human who pours scalding water over splotches of a poison oak rash.

This tree could not communicate very well, but it could communicate better than most trees. It had been top of its class in school. Some had attributed its success to its having been sprouted in whale dung instead of deer or elk or bear poop like most of the trees. The real idiots germinated in nothing but the dead matter of fallen trees.

The cause of this tree's exceptional intelligence was that it was the botanical aspect of the being of which the man sleeping in the closet and the bitch waiting to attack the intruder on the moon were also aspects.

Neither the sleeping man nor the high-strung bitch were aware of their unique connection with this tree. This tree that was afraid of grizzly bears and hoped it existed on Sakhalin Island instead of one of the Aleutians.

The tree was unaware of its connection with the crazy man and the bitch, but it was aware of forces outside itself that changed over time and that made it happy or sad for reasons the tree could not attribute to conditions in its immediate environment.

When the tree was inordinately hostile to the other trees or rocks or to the birds that landed in its branches, it was in close connection with the bitch on the moon. When it became inordinately neurotic and wanted to hide itself in the rectum of a humpback whale (its version of a womb) it empathized with the crazy man. And the tree would have been the first to tell the man that he was indeed crazy and not nearly as abnormal as he insisted—if, that is, the tree could communicate with the humans.

As the madman and the bitch were unaware of this connection with the tree, and as the tree was too much of an idiot to understand that it had a connection with two dysfunctional humans, it is left to me to tell you that the tree did in fact influence the lives, to some small degree at least, of the man who liked to sleep in closets and the woman who went to the moon because she was too much of a bitch to live on earth.

How it influenced their lives I cannot say explicitly, but perhaps you will discover it for yourself in the remainder of these pages.

Chapter 2

"Are you awake?" himself said to him.

"I have been awake for some time. How long was I asleep?"

"I don't know. I must have slept too."

The man had woken up in his dark closet.

"It is still very dark," he said to himself.

"You said you wanted it that way."

"Yes. I did."

"Now it is dark, and you don't know what time it is, and now you have slept and have no idea how much longer you have to wait."

"Yes. It is the pure detachment I was seeking. I feel my muddled head clearing already."

The furnace blower turned on. The first click shot through the wall and pierced the man's meditative state. The blower turned with a low but persistent hum that drowned out the voice of himself.

"I forgot about the furnace," the man said to himself. But himself did not answer.

The man had to retreat into his mind and converse with himself through inner dialogue.

The man wondered why he had picked that particular closet. He could have chosen another—and he would have if he he had thought about the furnace. The furnace closet was in the living room, and the bedroom closet and furnace closet shared the same wall. The wall next to the irritated man's head.

The man tried to converse with himself in his thoughts, but he began thinking too quickly, and the speed of his thoughts increased to the speed of the furnace blower, then his thought increased in multiples of the speed of the blower.

The man's anxiety increased too, but it did not hold at a steady rate with the blower. He became erratic once more like when he was out shopping too long—or at all—or when he had to join a cocktail party for the sake of his job—or for any reason.

His anxiety was tied to the furnace. First, he could feel his money draining out of his wallet with each turn of the blower and with each increase in heat that flowed from the vents. Winter. Not just dark, but cold.

Second, the furnace represented the grid. It was his duty as a citizen of the modern world to equip his home with a device for heating his home. What a wonderful invention the heat pump was. But it was a product of the collective society he was presently trying to avoid. Yes, he could not dispute the necessity of the furnace. And it was the most efficient way to heat his house, so it at least had that going for it.

But it was the necessity that annoyed him: the necessity that he had in common with all his fellow homeowners and citizens of his culture whom he wanted to forget—for at least one night.

The man did not like to think in exposition; he wanted to think in dialogue—out loud.

But he could not hear himself over the sound of the blower.

Then the blower turned off, but the man's mind continued to buzz.

The noises in his brain confused him. He tried to talk to himself, but everything came out distorted—or maybe he was only hearing it as distorted.

When a clear voice finally distinguished itself in his head, he realized his mother was calling to him from outside his bedroom door. The man froze. His brain stopped. All was silent.

His mother called his name again. She still used the diminutive form that embarrassed him so much. Had she heard him talking to himself?

"I know you're in there, now open up," she said.

The man wondered what she was doing there. It was her quilting night.

"I want to show you the new quilt I have finished."

The man was mortified. She probably had made it as a gift to him, and he would be obligated to display it prominently in the house. Most likely on the sofa.

"I made it for your birthday; now let me show it to you."

"Mom. I'm busy. Please show me another time." It had been a struggle, but he managed to put the words in what would pass as his own voice.

"Are you with a woman? I thought I heard voices."

"Yes."

"Can I meet her?"

"Next week. Please go."

"What's wrong with your voice? It sounds like it always did when I caught you talking to yourself in the closet."

"I'm fine, mom."

"Next week for dinner, then. I expect to meet the new one—though I'm sure this one won't last long either. And I'll leave the quilt on the sofa. I made it with that in mind."

The man listened to the sounds of his mother puttering around in the living room.

The front door closed. The car started and drove away.

"Will you take me to dinner with mom next week?" himself asked him.

"I'll try to get us out of it," he told himself.

"What will you do about the furnace blower interrupting us all night? You will leave the closet now, won't you?"

"No. I'm committed to staying here all night. I'll just put up with it."

"Who would you take to mom's if you can't get out of going? You don't know any women who would let herself be put through such torture."

"Don't go talking bad about mom now," he told himself.

"Don't get high and mighty just because you can spend a few hours alone in a dark closet," himself said.

"You know it's not right to talk bad about the dead."

The blower kicked on once more, and he and himself were sad as they thought about their long-dead mother.

* * *

The tree tried to get the attention of the nearby rock. It whispered as loudly as it could.

"Hey, rock."

The tree was not sure the rock had heard. So the tree repeated itself. But the tree still could not tell if the rock had heard.

The tree shrugged its branches and focused its attention on the big thing floating offshore. The big thing was a submarine, but the tree could not tell the difference between a submarine and a whale. The tree liked whales. A whale had been its surrogate mother.

The rock was grouchy. The rock wished it could have clearer communication with the tree. The tree always wanted to gab, and the rock would not have minded except every time the tree tried to get the rock's attention, it never took less than five minutes for the tree to recognize that the rock was responding. This made the rock grouchy.

The rock could see that the thing floating in the ocean nearby was a submarine and not a whale. The rock knew that the tree would think it was a whale, and the rock was sure that was why the tree was trying to get its attention.

The rock was very old. And even being so big and heavy, it had been around. Many storms had had their way with the rock.

"Dumb as a tree," the rock thought to itself. "And the so-called intelligent beings that populate this planet think a rock is dumb. They should try living next to a stand of trees for three hundred years."

The rock was also grouchy because the tide was up and at high tide only the top half of the rock was above water.

"I hate getting my feet wet," the rock thought.

The young tree stood alone near the water line.

There was no beach, just rock then dirt then the tree, and finally the path that separated the tree from the rest of the forest.

The rock watched the submarine.

"Mama," the tree sighed.

"It ain't your mama," the rock shouted.

"I didn't think it was exactly my mama."

"It's a submarine full of people and bombs. And even if it was a whale, and even if it was the whale that shit you out ten years ago, it still wouldn't be your mama."

The tree waved quietly in the wind.

"You're in a fine mood this morning," the tree said.

"It's high tide."

"That's no excuse," the tree teased the rock, "What's a submarine?"

"Never mind. It's as good as a whale," the rock said.

The tree squinted as best it could to try to distinguish features on the things that were different from a whale.

"I would like to think it was my mother."

"You would like to think anything is your mother. You don't understand. Trees come from other trees. Not from whales or submarines or rocks."

"Where did you come from?"

"I came from nowhere."

"You had to come from somewhere."

"Who says I had to? Who's been filling your puny brain with nonsense?"

"I just thought—"

"You thought nothing. I've always existed from forever."

"From the beginning of time?"

"From before the beginning of time."

"That's a long time."

"Not as long as these last ten years."

"I don't get it."

"You want my opinion?"

"About what?"

"Your mama was a fir tree on Sakhalin Island. Near the ocean. A fir cone drops from her branches and ends up in the ocean. It drifts in the ocean a long time. Then a whale one day swallows the fir cone in its giant gulp of seawater. The fir cone breaks down in its digestive tract, but the seeds move on until one day the seeds and the rest of the shit get shoved back out into the boundless sea. The waves carry the feces across the water where it is deposited on the shore, and some time later you sprout and somehow survive on this godforsaken island.

"This is not Sakhalin Island?"

"No."

"Kamchatka Peninsula?"

"No."

"What is it?"

"It's a place no one has ever visited before. It is a nameless spit of land in the miserable North Pacific."

"Who is God? And why has he forsaken us?"

"Just a figure of speech."

"What's this thing coming toward us from the whale?"

"It's not a whale. It's a submarine."

"You said it's as good as a whale."

"Call it a whale for all I care."

"So what's this thing coming from it?"

"A boat. With men."

"What do they want?"

"They want you to stop asking so many questions and observe and think for yourself."

The tree was silent. The tree tried to observe and think for itself. It did not do so well because a tree is very limited in its powers of observation and thought.

The men dragged the boat ashore. One of the men was a woman, and she stood on the rock and supervised.

* * *

The woman on the moon lunged from behind the boulder and attacked her intruder with her bare hands. She did not bother to get a good look at her victim. She simply attacked her victim as mercilessly and as brutally as possible.

She screamed and shouted, and even on a world with no atmosphere, her voice penetrated the souls of all beings who were within sight. Which consisted of exactly two people: herself and her dinner.

The woman tore at the flesh. She gouged out the eyes. Hair came out in bunches in her fists.

Within an hour, the woman had entirely devoured the intruder.

The woman was almost satiated. She had not realized how hungry she had become. She could not even remember the last time she had eaten people food.

The woman lay down and slept.

When she woke up, she found that she had been bound securely to a rock. She was bound at the wrists, and her arms were stretched behind the rock.

Three women stood before her. The sun was behind them, so the woman saw only their silhouettes.

"Who are you? And what do you want?" the woman demanded.

The middle of the three women spoke. Her voice sounded just like the woman's.

"We are physical manifestations of your psyche."

"Bullshit," the woman roared.

The three women turned so the sun showed more of their faces. They looked exactly like the woman.

"Who sent you?"

"You did," the women said in unison.

"I don't know what you are talking about."

The woman strained at the cords that bound her until blood trickled from where they cut her. She pulled until she felt her shoulders would pop out of their sockets. But before they did, the cords gave way.

As the woman rose to her feet, her three captors attacked her.

For two days the four women battled and bled. They did not stop to eat or drink. They did not stop to sleep. They did not stop at night, and they did not stop at day.

At nightfall of the second day of fighting, the woman yelled out for everyone to stop.

They stopped. But they were on their guard.

"I did not send for you."

"Yes, you did," the leader of the three said between her broken teeth.

"How?"

"Our man is very limited. He can enter his closet and speak with himself in two different voices, but that is all. You, on the other hand, have grown strong enough to split your personality out as separate beings. Not only can we talk with you, but we can interact with you as you would with anyone else."

"I don't want anyone else. I want to be alone."

And with that, the woman attacked the leader of the three other women, and the battle raged for three days this time.

The woman could not gain an advantage, but neither could her assailants.

"Why do you attack me?" the woman asked.

"Look what you did to the first of us."

"Who was that?"

"The one whom you devoured."

"That was one of you?"

"One of you to be precise. You didn't recognize anything about her?"

"You are trespassing on my domain. I will drive you off or devour you like I did the other."

"Then you will only create more of us."

The second woman touched the third woman on the shoulder seductively.

"Stop that," the woman said.

The second woman drew closer to the third and kissed her cheek.

The woman stepped in between them. She slapped each of their faces but resisted attacking them further.

"You could not have come from me," she said. "That slut male must have sent you."

The leader of the three women stood with her feet apart and her arms crossed under her breasts.

"You are in denial."

"Must I continue this fight?" the woman asked. "I will fight to the end if you don't stop your insolence."

The first woman smiled at the woman. She cupped her own breasts and pinched her nipples.

The woman felt her own nipples harden. She also felt her own resolve harden.

The woman had enough. She ran away from the other three. She ran across the bottom of the crater and up to the top of the surrounding ridge. When she looked back down into the crater, the three women were running after her, but they were spread out. The five days of battle had worn each one differently. The third woman had not fought very hard. She was fresher and in the lead. A short distance behind her was the second woman. The leader had been the strongest foe, and she had fought hardest too. She was far behind the other two.

Collectively, they were the woman's equal. But individually, none of them stood a chance.

The woman entered the crater once more.

She only devoured the first woman she came across. She easily subdued the other two. She bound them and preserved them for the future in her food storing shelter.

Others would be coming. She was sure of that now, and she wanted to build up her strength for the coming war. She was not preparing for a battle but rather an apocalypse. They would come in more numbers and with more intelligence. She would have to prove to be superior in every category. And she wanted it more than anything she had wanted in her life.

Chapter 3

The tree turned its attention to the sky. The big sky. The big blue sky. The big blue sky above the tree and the rock and the other trees and the island and the ocean and the earth.

The big blue sky with the moon staring down from above.

The men gathered around the tree with their instruments. A woman stood on the rock. The rock tried to speak to the tree, but it could not while the woman stood on it. She muffled the rock's voice, and the tree had enough trouble hearing the rock anyway.

The trees across the path from the tree were curious about the people and the funny looking whale and the tree's preoccupation with the moon.

"You really think you're superior, don't you?" one of them said.

The tree said nothing. The tree was preoccupied with the moon. The tree was also preoccupied with the people and their instruments. The tree began to feel aroused in the same way it did when the grizzly bear clawed at its back.

"Superiority complex for sure," another tree said.

"What do you expect from something that came from whale shit?" said another.

The tree wondered why the moon always looked different from one day to the next. The tree did not have an astronomical model to work from. The tree also did not know that the tides were related to the moon.

The tree liked the blue sky. The tree liked the moon. But the tree liked the stormy gray sky even better.

The tree liked to sway in the fierce winds. The tree liked to feel every fiber of its being stretch under the force of a storm.

The tree also liked the cold. The extreme cold of the North Pacific in winter. The other trees said the tree was a cold-blooded tree. It liked the feeling of hibernating in the winter. The other trees said it was not normal for an evergreen to go dormant in the winter and to lose its needles and stand naked on the shore of the ocean.

The tree liked being singular. The tree liked being naked. The tree liked hibernating in the winter. The tree sometimes even thought of itself as a bear.

"I am the grizzly tree! Born from the union of a great whale and a grizzly bear!" But the tree never said such a thing out loud. The others would certainly laugh to hear such non-sense from the tree. They already alienated the tree for its other singular features, behaviors, and attitudes. And the rock would have certainly given the tree a lecture on the impossi-bility of such a union in the natural world. The tree did not give a damn about what was possible in the natural world!

One of the men drilled a hole in the tree. He inserted a probe that was attached to an instrument that another man held.

"That tickles," the tree said.

The tree regretted saying anything at all.

"Are you trying to talk to the people now?" one of the oth-er trees asked.

"Hey, Morton, the whale-child says it tickles when the people do that to it," another tree said.

Morton was an old birch tree that had managed to exist among the firs. Morton was special in no other way. In fact, most of the trees that grew near the ocean no longer even thought of Morton as different from them in any way.

"I said long ago, from the day that thing sprouted from the dung of a whale, that nothing good would come from having that stick in our midst," Morton said.

The people with their instruments worked diligently, but one of them did mention to the others that the trees made an awful lot of noise that day considering there was no wind.

Morton told the others that it was the people communicating in their noisy language that accounted for such a strange noise on the windless day.

The people did not consider that the trees were communicating with each other in any kind of language—noisy or not—so they did not consider that such a strange noise on the windless day was in fact trees communicating with each other.

The people did not consider such things because they did not think it was possible for trees to communicate.

In the deepest depths of her heart, though, the woman who stood on the rock did consider such a possibility. Not as a possibility that might actually be true, but as a poetic possibility.

The woman began composing a poem about the conversations a forest might have on a sunny, warm day devoid of wind on an island in the North Pacific. She was way off on her interpretation, but that was because as a human she did not have the imagination to conceive of what an actual conversation among the trees would have consisted of. But to her credit, she did imagine the poetic possibility of such a conversation—if not the actual possibility.

And the woman buried this poem and this imagined poetic possibility deep in her heart. She knew the others would consider her crazy for entertaining such a notion, and she did not want to sully her sterling reputation as a dependable science officer.

"Don't think you are crazy," the tree said to the woman. But the woman did not hear. She heard but did not understand. She did not speak the language of the trees—even the language of such a precocious and superior tree as the whale-child that thought of itself as the grizzly tree.

But the woman was happy. Happy in a way she could not account for—and she did not want to try to account for it.

* * *

The blower stopped.

The man listened as his thoughts tumbled into place in the silence.

In the silence the man finally felt a moment of peace. Not complete peace, but the first taste of the peace he had sought when he had entered the closet.

"Do I dare call it sanity?" he asked himself.

"Temporary sanity perhaps," himself replied.

The man listened deep into the darkness. He could hear the cars out on the freeway. They were too far away to disturb his peace. They did not disturb his peace, that is, as long as he did not let himself think about how the freeway was connected to every other freeway, and to every road and boulevard and avenue and street and driveway. Another grid.

But he did not think about the grid, so it did not disturb his peace.

"You did not account for everything, did you?" himself asked him when he felt the urge to pee.

"No. Maybe I should consider this one a trial run. Get an idea of all the obstacles and take better care next time to eliminate them."

"Just run to the bathroom and come back."

"No. I have an idea."

The man stood up in the closet the best he could, fighting with his shirts and ties and the few pants he kept on hangers.

He had a pleasant sensation of his half-erect penis hanging between his legs.

"Next time you should bring a woman into the closet with you," himself told him. "That would eliminate many obstacles."

"I'll take care of it after I pee. If I take care of it myself, that will eliminate the larger obstacles of having to find a woman who would join me in here."

"How will you pee without leaving the closet? Do you have a jar or a bucket in here?"

"Not a jar, but I'll have to remember one next time."

"You're not going to just piss on the floor, are you?"

"Nothing so dirty as that. I told you I'm not completely crazy."

The man pulled a blanket down from the shelf above the rod that held his clothes hangers. He folded the blanket thickly and his erection grew.

"So you'll piss on a blanket?"

"At least it's not one of mom's quilts."

"How will you piss with that hard on?"

The man ignored himself. He tried to relax. But he could not relax. His erection grew harder.

"See what I mean about having a woman in here? She'd be quite useful," himself told him.

"Only for fifteen minutes. After that I'd face the same old problems as ever. No, better take care of it myself and leave those problems for others."

The man thought about a couple of women he had met recently. The longer he thought about them, the more flaccid his penis became. Soon he only had to pee again.

"You'd really do it when you have a perfectly functional toilet twenty feet away?" himself asked him.

"It is part of the freedom I came into the closet to find. The toilet represents convention. It represents utilities and the interconnectedness of humans with the resources that support our basic necessities."

"For good reason!"

"One time won't give me hepatitis."

The man was much more relaxed now that he had discovered such a banal topic to discuss with himself.

At first the pee dribbled out in a few drops. He stopped himself out of habit.

"You can't go through with it, can you?"

"Watch."

The man closed his eyes and gave himself up to the darkness. He began to pee as though he was deep in the forest behind a tree.

The urine pooled up on the blanket and soon the stream of pee sounded like it did when he peed into a full toilet. The man wondered if the blanket was not exactly the kind that would absorb moisture readily. But he continued to pee freely.

When the man finished peeing, he was relieved. He felt relieved and he felt free. He was more at peace than ever.

"You better make sure it didn't soak through the blanket and onto the carpet below," himself told him.

The man ran his hand under the blanket. He felt some dampness on the back of this hand from the bottom of the blanket, but the carpet was dry.

"Now what will you do with the blanket?" himself asked him. "It will continue to soak through."

The man put the blanket on top of the stack of blankets he kept on the shelf.

"Are you sure you didn't throw that on top of one of mom's quilts?"

The man ignored himself. He was almost happy. He wondered what others would say if they knew what he had done, and he did not care. He was pleased that he had done something most would not think to do ever in their lives.

The man lay back down on the floor. He pulled the dry blanket over both him and himself. He placed his head on the soft pillow.

The man was wide-awake, and he was pleased. He knew at that moment that he had what it would take to make it all the way until morning.

On that thought alone, the man's erection returned, and when it was hard enough, he took care of it with much joy.

* * *

The sun went down, and the woman on the moon waited.

The woman waited in her shelter for the next wave of attackers, intruders, and whores. None had come since the three women earlier. But more were on their way. She could feel it.

The woman was not afraid. The woman was ready. She would vanquish whole armies of her own invention if it came to that.

The woman knew she was a bitch, but she also knew she was not crazy. Certainly she was not schizophrenic—she was not and the man was not.

The woman thought about the man. She had not felt much from him for a long time, but whenever she thought she was free of him, she felt a tug against her will that reminded her that somewhere in the depths of the deep depths, the fish was still on the line. The only problem was that this fish held her on the line, and she could not get free of it no matter how hard she tried.

And she tried hard. Harder than hard. She was the most competent being she knew, and it was the one thing she had not succeeded in doing. She had always been a bitch, but this made her even more of a bitch, and she knew she would be such a bitch until she had swallowed this fish and the earth and the moon and the sun and spit out the hook and swivel and sinkers and line. Then she would not be such a bitch anymore because she would be free. But she knew that even in the best of times she would still be a bitch. She just would not be such a bitch as at this moment.

The woman liked to think about how much of a bitch she was. It was the source of her strength—so she thought anyway. She would not learn for a long time that the source of her strength was her peculiar and particular human strain of mammalian adaptability. She was the manifestation of the survival instinct. She would be the queen bitch until the end of time if it meant self-preservation, and to hell with anyone else who might be preserved or destroyed in the process.

Yes, some are preserved in the process. Some ride along in the wake that her great disturbance caused in the placid waters of time. Some are preserved such as the fish. The slut fish on the end of the line that she could not cast off. Perhaps even the whole of the cosmos existed in the wake that followed the bitch through time. She could consider such a possibility from her subjective point of view. In her most generous frame of mind, she would imagine all the worlds existing from the composite energy of all the bitches in the universe, but she was the queen bitch, and all others existed according to her own being.

And all things ceased to exist according to her being as well. She took neither pleasure nor pain from any of it. It was simply the way things were and always would be. It was her duty, and she did it well.

She wanted to eat. The woman wanted to eat, but she was not hungry. If she were hungry then she would need to eat. But she did not need to eat. She did not need to eat, but she wanted to eat.

She wanted to eat because she knew they were coming and she wanted to make sure she had the strength to overcome anything they sent against her. She was not paranoid. She knew she was not paranoid. She knew in the same way that she knew that neither she nor the man were schizophrenic. She knew. She knew but she also knew that she had to prepare. She was not paranoid, she was preparing. Preparing for all that her cosmos would send against her because she knew in the deepest depth of her depths that her cosmos was against her, and she would not rest until she had destroyed it, but not destroy it completely, only destroy it as it was, and she would make it as she wanted and needed it to be. No more fish and no more lives. After that she would no longer need to be a bitch. At least not such a bitch. If only they would give her what she wanted without fighting about it, then she would not have to be such a bitch to begin with.

Yes, it was time for something to eat.

The woman left her sleeping shelter and went to her food storing shelter. She had an appetite for the leader of the three women. That one had been a bitch in training while the other two women had been sheep. Followers. Chattel.

The woman had an appetite for bitch, and that almost-bitch who had trained hard and had perhaps almost earned her stripes was just what the woman had a taste for.

But neither of the two bodies she had stored for future consumption were in the food storing shelter.

The woman wondered if they had returned to life and run away. But she knew that was impossible. She knew that such bodies were perishable, and they could not be preserved. The field of battle was the only place she could enjoy such a feast. She knew this, but she had not known it when she had killed them in the crater. She had fully expected them to nourish her when she wanted it.

And she was still hungry. No, not hungry. She did not need to eat. She still wanted to eat. She wanted to fortify herself against the future.

She tried to conjure a new being that she could kill and devour. She tried hard. She tried hard, and she succeeded.

Outside the food storing shelter, her snack approached.

Chapter 4

The tree was lonely. The people had returned to their whale. It was night. The moon was not up. The sun was not up. The tide was not up.

All the other trees slept. They slept, so they did not tease or mock or ridicule the tree, but the tree did not mind their teasing and mocking and ridicule. The tree did not like the silence. But the tree could stand the silence more than it could stand sleeping, so it stayed awake in the silence instead of sleeping like the other trees.

"I liked that woman," the rock whispered.

"Why do you whisper?" the tree asked.

"I always whisper at night. I don't want to wake the other trees and rocks."

"Don't you sleep?"

"I'm a rock. Why would I need to sleep?"

"You don't seem so grouchy tonight."

"I'm in love."

"You don't need to sleep, but you can love?"

"Didn't you see that woman?"

"How can you love one of those creatures?"

"Love is never a question of how. It's only a question of is."

"She stood on you the whole time they were here."

"Yes, she could feel my infatuation."

"Have you ever loved one of them before?"

"Once. In Ecuador."

"What happened?"

"None of your business. It's not polite to ask such questions."

"Sorry."

The rock felt a wave lap up against it. The tide was way out, but even so a wave sometimes managed to reach the rock.

"Do you think those people will return in the morning?" the tree asked the rock.

"It's hard to say. They might even return after they eat their dinner."

"I've never seen one of these people before. I hadn't even heard of them before today. What do they want with us? With me? What did that woman want with you?"

"People are the most unpredictable creatures on this planet. It's best if you avoid them completely."

"But you have loved one, and you are falling in love again," the tree said.

"So I know what I am talking about!"

The tree felt its roots dig deeper into the soil.

"How can I avoid them if I am rooted to this spot?"

"Just try to avoid attracting attention to yourself."

"What did I do to attract their attention today?"

"I don't know. You've always been an odd one. Maybe even the people have discovered your oddity too."

"I don't try to behave oddly. I simply try to behave as naturally as possible."

"Then you are naturally odd."

"Is it a bad thing?"

"Doesn't hurt me any."

"You are odd too?"

"No, I'm a perfectly normal rock. What I meant was that it doesn't hurt me any for you to be such an oddity."

"Do you think I could fall in love with that woman too?"

"Leave my woman alone," the rock said. "Why? Did you feel something for her?"

The rock began to wish it had some tide in which to hide. It was reluctant to share its feelings so openly with the tree.

"No, but I think I could if I tried."

"Then try to love one of those men, if you don't mind, and leave the woman to me."

"I only wondered because I felt that only the woman could communicate with me. The men were too determined to do what they came to do and then forget about me."

"Then wait for your grizzly bear to return. Leave my woman alone."

The tree swayed in a freshening wind. It danced. The tree danced in the freshening wind, and it wished the woman was there to dance with it. It wished for the woman in spite of what the rock had said. It wished for the woman because the tree felt that the men did not dance in the way a woman could. The men could not dance with a tree the way the tree liked to dance. But the tree was sure this woman could dance in the way the tree liked to dance.

The tree plotted to steal away the heart of the woman from the ugly, stationary rock.

"What are you thinking?" the rock asked the tree.

The tree said nothing. It looked at the stars, and it danced in the freshening breeze.

"What are you doing? What are you thinking?" the rock persisted.

"I'm thinking I will try to sleep."

"Maybe you are not so odd after all."

The tree did not sleep, though. The tree thought about the woman. And then, as though having been summoned by the tree, the woman appeared.

"What's this?" the tree asked the rock.

"Another boat."

"It only has two people in it. A man and the woman."

"We have competition," the rock said.

"Maybe they came to examine me again."

"In your dreams. You don't know anything about how these creatures behave at night!"

* * *

The woman on the moon knew something was wrong right away. It was too easy. When she had stepped out of her food storing shelter to confront the intruder, she saw that it was her mother, and she devoured the beast instantly and without a struggle.

It had been too easy, and the meal was entirely unsatisfying. Had she needed to eat—instead of merely wanting to eat—she would have starved on such fare.

She was alert. She had expected another aggressive Amazon, and she had looked forward to the feast. But they had played a trick on her.

First they had tried to take her by force, but now they had turned to guile. It was a warning. Nothing would come easily. She was not one to be taken easily in any manner, with force or with guile, and they would know that very well.

And then they scored their first point. She entered her sleeping shelter and found an infant lying among the soft blankets on her austere bed.

She could not devour the child. She screamed into the black void above and felt herself splitting into two then four then eight then fifteen pieces. The last sixteenth that refused to split was the soul of the hearty bitch that would stitch the woman back into the fearsome wench that she had worked so hard to become.

Thin streams of molten tears flowed from her eyes of rage. Her mouth dripped with succulent appetite, but she could not satisfy the depths of her desires to annihilate the quivering pile of flesh tucked warmly in the swaddled bed.

The infant had brown eyes. Brown, intelligent eyes. Intelligent eyes that were already measuring the newly maternal being for the infant's own breakfast.

The woman was ready to throw the infant into the outer reaches of oblivion, but the blankets fell away, and the woman saw that the infant was a girl. A male child she could have devoured, or at the very least thrown into the outer reaches of oblivion, but a girl child gave her pause.

That maternal appetizer had been a trick indeed. She had been too aggressive against her own mother and in so doing had absorbed the spirit of her mother—just as they had intended.

But she would not give in. She would not yield permanently to the maternal instinct. She would pay for her indiscriminate actions, but she would grow stronger and smarter, and she would triumph in the end.

The woman lifted the infant into the cradle of her arms.

Immediately, the infant latched on to the woman's breast with its mouth and began sucking.

The woman pulled the infant away, but the infant held firm. The woman felt the bile that fueled her ambition drain out through her breast and into the little monster she had allowed to get so close.

The woman closed her eyes and forced her breast to stop the feeding.

"Why do you starve me, mama?" the infant asked the woman.

"I am not your mama, and you will not starve, you vile creature."

The infant began to cry.

The woman wrapped the infant in the blankets and left it on her bed. She stepped out of her sleeping shelter and ran until she could no longer hear the crying.

The woman considered her options, but she could not think of any at the moment. She could not destroy the infant, nor could she feed and nurture it. She would have to destroy it, but she would not be able to destroy it until she had recovered her nasty self that was currently shattered.

The woman became even angrier when she realized what had caused the dampness between her legs. Her sudden confrontation with motherhood had stimulated other physical systems associated with motherhood—physical systems that she had neglected for a long time.

"I am a slut now too," the woman said in her shame.

She lay back on the soft moon dust and looked at the stars above. She fought in her mind to dispense with the erotic chemical surging through her. Her antidote to the substance of human weakness was depleted, and she longed for the strength of mind she had counted on and that had preserved her in her abstinence for so long.

It was too much. She had been defeated, but not permanently. She could drop her guard now in full retreat and recuperate for tomorrow's battle. Let them think they were further ahead than they were. A nubile young woman materialized from nowhere to serve the woman's needs.

The woman spread her legs. But when the young woman touched her, the woman rose up and devoured her whole.

The woman on the moon fell asleep.

* * *

"It is not as easy as it sounds," he told himself.

He and himself were suspended in the silence of the dark closet, suspended in the peace he had sought.

"But they exist for a reason, and if not to help those like you, than what is that reason?" himself replied.

"It sounds good, of course. It sounds plausible. I cannot deny that the profession exists and that it at least claims to exist for the reason you say. But I disagree on one small point. It exists precisely to help those who are not like me."

"And what is that distinction? You cannot be saying that they exist to help those who are normal."

"Yes and no. Yes it exists to help those who are normal. Those who inherently feel the plausible foundation of the profession as a whole, and who think nothing of looking for succor from such sources. And no, it does not exist to help those who are normal: it exists to help those who are normally normal but through normal adverse circumstances they hit a few bumps and are knocked off their horse. They are normal people with normal problems, and the profession's normal methods help them get back on their horse."

"Don't you want to get back on your horse?"

"I never had a horse. Or I was knocked off it so long ago that I wouldn't know what to do with one even if I had the help."

"Certainly the profession has help for someone like you. You can't think you are as special as that. After a century of development I'm sure the profession has seen it all."

"You are being generous—as you should—in considering this point of view. But consider my point of view for a moment," he told himself.

"Okay, what is your point of view?" himself replied, and himself sat quietly and waited to hear his point of view.

"First I must pick one. Right? I must choose one. Maybe three or four will give me an initial consultation, but what can you learn about someone in thirty minutes?"

"They are trained and experienced in delving to the core of your issues, and they do much better than you might think at analyzing a client in a brief time."

The man sat silently. He was getting angry.

"You don't understand. I mean it is not enough time for me to learn much about them and to choose which one I would hire. I don't understand the obsequious attitude the clients or patients or cases bring to such relationship. It is like they think that because something is wrong with them and because the clinician is a paid expert, then they must yield their identity to the therapist. Here I am, doctor, fix me. When I want someone to help me with something, and I pay them for that help, then they are working for me. I know I am not a good boss, at least in administrative matters, so such interviews are particularly painful to me, and they only heighten my sense of inadequacy. And no! I will not outsource my sanity."

Himself felt like he was on a roll, and himself remained silent while the man thought.

"They are prepared to deal with normal abnormality, not abnormal normality," he finally said.

Himself let this statement pass as sheer rhetoric.

"Look," the man said, "they want you to talk. They believe in talking. It isn't like when you take your car in and they hook it up to the computers and the computers identify exactly what's wrong and why. Instead, you go in and sit down and a clinician says, 'What's your problem?' and you think you have an hour, and you have so much to say, and before you think you have even begun, they tell you it's been fifty minutes. So you prepare to wind down the last ten minutes, but at that moment, they shut you up and usher you to the exit room where they take your hundred and fifty dollars. And you ask what about the hour, and they say they need ten minutes to prepare for the next appointment. You ask for twenty-five dollars back, but they say they spent ten minutes before the session preparing for you. You ask how they prepared when they had nothing to go on except the initial consultation three weeks ago. They say they always can find enough to go on. And you are sure they can at a hundred fifty an hour. But when you ask for a conclusion or for the results of their preparation and training and experience, they say it is better if you find the answers yourself."

"You expect too much from them," himself said.

"I expect too much from everybody, and particularly my-self. But for a hundred fifty an hour, don't you think it's hard to expect too little?"

"Maybe you should become one yourself then."

"You didn't hear me, did you? It's fundamentally flawed, the talking. When the problem is that you cannot put such things into words, and the only line of communication is talk-ing, then there is an absolute disconnect and no hope for pro-gress."

"You are very good with words," himself told him.

"It's not the words, goddamnit. It's the relationship. The problems are in your head when you are alone. You know your appointment is on this day and at this time, and you know you can pump yourself up for the performance they draw you into. You can do it for fifty minutes every three weeks. You can even look forward to it. But when it's all over, you know nothing good came of it, and you are left with your hideous wasteland for the next three weeks before you can do it again."

"They never see you as you are in your private moments," himself said in agreement.

"Now you are getting it. Their very presence takes you out of your abnormally normal frame of mind and it appears you have no problems. It's another manifestation of the Uncer-tainty Principle. But there is no uncertainty when it comes time to pay the bill, or when they write up your case study for their annual conferences.

Himself was glad the blower had come on. Himself was getting tired.

Chapter 5

The sun rose over the far side of the moon.

The woman woke where she slept in the moon dust when the sun shined on her back.

She still was not cold.

The woman was satisfied in her appetite. The nubile young woman had come at the right time. The woman had not been hungry, but she had been aware that she needed food to prepare for battle. She did not want to become hungry at the height of a crisis.

She was not tired, but she had slept. She had slept to prepare herself for the coming battle. She did not want to become tired at the height of crisis.

They had left her alone while she slept. She had expected that they would leave her alone, and they had. But she was sure they had not forgotten about her. They were preparing, just as she was preparing. Perhaps they had slept too.

The woman sat up and looked at her sleeping shelter in the distance. What had they done with the infant? Anything?

It had not been her infant, she sure of that. That greedy sucking pig could not have come from her womb. Neither the womb of her body nor the womb of her mind.

The woman concluded that in truth she had liked the second of the three women from the day before, if only a little.

She regretted that the two specimens she had stored away had disappeared. She would have liked to have had the first for breakfast and the second for something else.

The woman did not like to waste her time on possibilities. They distracted her from the present—the reality that she was determined to conquer. She put the two women out of her mind and steeled herself for the coming skirmish.

The door to the sleeping shelter opened. The infant crawled out the door and onto the surface of the moon.

The sleeping shelter was on the other side of the crater from the woman. It would take much time for the infant to reach the woman. The woman was determined not to run. She would confront this problem like she confronted every problem—head on and with no mercy.

The woman set up a fire pit with a rotisserie.

The male approached from behind the nearby boulder just as the woman sensed he would. He was not much of a man. He was a young man—not more than a boy really.

The woman asked the boy to start the fire. He said he could not. He said a fire would not burn on the moon on account of the lack of oxygen.

The woman asked the boy to try anyway.

The boy was lost.

The woman started the fire and put the boy on the spit.

The boy said that the fire was not hot but that the stick through his body hurt a great deal.

The woman dispensed with the fire. It had been strictly for mood anyway. She turned her gaze on the boy, and he said that was much warmer. Then he said it was hot. Then he said it was too hot. Then he could not say anything else because he was dead, but his fat sizzled on the moon rocks below him in the fire pit, and the woman was pleased.

The infant approached, crawling on hands and knees.

"Who are you?" the infant asked the woman.

"I was going to ask you the same thing," the woman said.

They split the wishbone. The infant won.

"What did you wish for?"

"If I tell you it won't come true."

The infant crawled closer to the woman, but the woman stepped away from the infant.

"Mama."

"I am not your mama, and you know it."

"I wish that you were my mama."

The woman stopped retreating and the infant drew closer.

"You are not my child."

"I wish I were. Why can't you kill me and eat me like you do the others?"

"Because I know who you are," the woman said.

"You know they did not send me," the infant said.

"Yes, I know."

And the woman yielded.

The infant began eating at the woman's fingers.

"You are me," the woman said. "You are me as an infant, and you are my chance to start over again."

The infant did not say anything. It was busy consuming the woman's flesh.

"Do you feel the connection to that slut man as you ingest me?"

"He is part of us. He is part of me. It is not a connection. It is an aspect. An inherent aspect."

The infant consumed legs and torso, all the way up to the neck.

"I hoped he would go away," the woman's head said.

"I have accepted him. He is at peace."

"Are you at peace?"

"Now I am, but I won't be after I absorb your mind. Your mind is too strong and corrupt for me to absorb it and remain healthy."

And the infant ate the woman's neck and head and brains. And the infant absorbed the woman's mind. And the infant transformed into the woman, and the woman looked up at the sun and screamed and asked what she had ever done wrong to deserve this.

* * *

The tree observed the man and the woman as they got out of the boat. The boat banged against the rock.

"That must have hurt," the tree said.

"Not as much as what will happen next," the rock said.

But what the rock feared would happen did not happen right away.

"It looks like they will torture me first," the rock said.

The tree was used to the rock complaining by now and had learned to ignore its whining.

The man held the boat for the woman, and the tree noticed that the woman disembarked with much grace.

The man and the woman had instruments, and they used the instruments to analyze the tree just as the larger group of people had done earlier in the day.

"See, they have come for me," the tree said. The tree did not gloat. It said this merely as a statement of fact.

"It's something called a perfunctory activity," the rock said. But even though the tree had not been gloating, the rock had taken the tree's comment close to heart. The rock could often be over-sensitive about such things. The rock had replied as smugly as it could, but the tree missed the emotional content of the message.

"What's perfunctory?"

"It was their excuse to go off alone away from the others on the submarine."

"The whale?"

"Your mama."

The tree knew that the rock was teasing this time.

"Why would they want to use their analysis of me as an excuse to go away from my mama?"

The rock did not have eyes, but if it had eyes, it would have rolled them.

"Keep watching," was all the rock said.

Now at this point you might be thinking that the man and the woman were the man in the closet and the woman on the moon. Perhaps as a flashback to a time when they had met, or a flash-forward to a scene where the tree connects them as I promised it would. But no. The man in the closet still lies in the closet, though time for him passes at a different rate than it passes for the woman on the moon and the tree. And the woman on the moon is still on the moon fighting with her inner bitch that has taken over her whole being, and her time passes at a different rate than time passes for the tree and the man. And the man in the closet and the woman on the moon are still two aspects of the same being of which the tree is a third aspect.

How the time passes differently for the man in the closet and the woman on the moon and the tree on the nameless, godforsaken island in the North Pacific not even the tree could explain. It is true that I did say the tree—and its forebears—could have written Einstein's paper on capillary action long before 1905, but that is because a tree's entire life support system depends on such a process. And they can even claim, without too much exaggeration, that they invented the whole concept. But they are as incapable as you or I are of understanding the finer points of another one of Einstein's 1905 papers, on special relativity—you know $E=mc^2$. And that is not even to mention that the actual description of why time passes differently for all three aspects of the same being was not described until 1924 by Einstein's field equation—you know $G_{\mu\nu}=8\pi T_{\mu\nu}$—commonly called—even among the trees— the general theory of relativity.

How time passes differently for each according to the laws of general relativity when none of the three aspects of our protagonists are moving at significant fractions of the speed of light (relative to each other) I cannot say. I mean I cannot because I do not know, not because I am not allowed to. I would tell you if I knew, but I do not know. But it does not bother me that I do not know and cannot say, so I hope you are not bothered as well.

The man and the woman finished the work with their instruments, and they put the instruments in the boat. They did not put themselves in the boat.

The man and the woman sat at the base of the tree and began what someone as naïve as the tree would call kissing but what someone as wizened as the rock would call foreplay.

"Look, they are kissing," the tree said.

"Call it what you want," the rock said. "Aren't you a little young to know about such things? And you only learned to-day that these creatures called people even exist."

"But trees kiss too."

"Poppycock," said the rock.

"What are they doing now?"

"Close your eyes. I bet you trees don't do anything like that."

"Why do I feel funny all over?"

"Because you are a degenerate."

"I think it's sweet."

"It is disgusting."

"You are just jealous."

"Maybe I am. That woman is beautiful."

"The man is lovely too," the tree said.

"I wouldn't know about that," the rock replied.

"Is it over so quickly? I wanted it to go on and on."

"They have not done such a thing for a long time."

"Why do they use that instrument on old Morton?"

"They are marking their place. A heart and their initials will be embedded in Morton's skin forever. Haha. Morton!"

"But why don't they mark me?"

"You like to have all the attention for yourself, don't you?"

"I just thought if they did such a thing next to me then—"

"It only means one thing: Tomorrow they'll be back with the others, and they don't want the others to see what they've done."

* * *

The man had become used to the blower by this time, and he continued talking to himself even though he knew himself was getting tired.

He had never talked to himself for such a long time. His throat was dry.

"Why don't you stop talking and just think for awhile," himself said to him.

"I've almost reached the end," he said.

"You should remember to store some water next time. It's another lesson learned. Add it to the list."

"It's a dilemma," he said to himself. "The more I drink, the more I'd have to pee."

"But next time you'll have a jar."

"It's very rational. Don't you think I'm too rational to be crazy?"

"You are rational when they expect you to be irrational. That is why you are crazy."

"Abnormal."

"I won't argue," himself said.

"Why? Because you agree or because you don't think it would do any good?"

Himself rolled his eyes at him and stayed silent.

"It's really not about reason or irrationality," he continued. "It's about politeness. I'm just too polite to go crazy in the classic sense. Big, dramatic scene, hurting those who love you. I mean, if you pick your moments wisely, you can go completely nuts once in a while and no one's the wiser. That's the only way I've been able to maintain any semblance of sanity these last many years.

"Polite, yes. Very polite," himself said to him. "You are very polite, but not very friendly."

"That's just asking too much."

"And that's what you are afraid the professionals would demand of you too, isn't it?"

"You drag me back onto that topic? Look, it's the problem of finding the right one. You think they're all interchangeable? Just look through the directory and any one will do?"

"You try a couple and go from there. As you said before, they'll all give you an initial consultation."

"Okay, and then you find that perhaps nineteen in twenty are unsuitable. What do you say to those nineteen? You enter a relationship, no matter how briefly, and when you find that they aren't good for much more than holding your hand when you've fallen off your horse, what do you tell them? They are so confident in themselves and their methods and their—what's the word, industry?—that anything you might say to suggest they are not suitable entirely spoils the atmosphere."

"And they set their fees according to their confidence, not their competence," himself said trying to commiserate.

"Exactly. But I do not doubt that their confidence is well earned. I mean, it seems quite normal—in the strict sense of the word again—for people in this culture to think nothing of paying a hundred fifty an hour to have someone hold their hand when they've fallen off their horse. So that sets the rate. If you have deeper problems then you can expect to really pay for it—not just in money but in time and effort just trying to find someone who can do more than hold the hands of those who have fallen off their horse."

"And you don't have much money to begin with," himself reminded him. But he already knew this; he did not need to be reminded.

"And when financial problems—or more precisely dysfunction in integrating into one's economic milieu—is a major part of the problem, then paying for help, and paying just to go on the journey to find the help, only exacerbates the problem.

"Well, it gives them more problems to fix when you do find someone adequate. Job security, you know?" himself said.

"It's like another field of endeavor in which the practitioners are willing for about the same hourly rate to give you all the help they promise will be helpful to you."

"Why don't you try that instead? It would likely fill a void that is directly related to your happiness," himself said.

"It is the same problem though. How do you find the right one? And how to afford it? I mean once in three weeks is not enough. If I can't have it once or twice a day, then better have none at all."

"You are just better off taking care of yourself," himself told him. Himself decided that taking his side and reassuring him was the quickest way to calm him down and shut him up.

"Yes, even my insanity. My abnormality, rather. I know when I need to go into the closet."

"But will you know when to get out?"

The man was silent for a time.

"I'm not worried about it. I have my alarm set. I will wake like any other morning and prepare for work," he said.

"But with a new outlook."

"A fresh outlook. Self-control will be my method. Not talk."

"They will think that you think you are superior," himself pointed out, daring once more to confront him.

"I will transcend talk. I will create. I create myself first in the crucible of this closet, and then I create a life that transcends their talk and their fees; no, it devours their talk and their fees. I will say nothing about my superiority. I will be modest and remain silent. But they will recognize it. They will recognize it but they will not understand it."

The man and himself remained quiet for an hour after this outburst.

Chapter 6

The woman on the moon tried to remember. She tried to remember anything from the past. Anything that might give her a hint as to what had happened and why. Whom could she blame?

But the woman could not remember anything. She was entirely a bitch, and a bitch lives only for the moment. No regret, no perspective. Pure reactionary reaction.

The woman tried to contemplate the future. The future of herself. The future of the moon. The future of this man she was bound to.

The moment was all that mattered. She had forgotten already her scream of self-loathing and self-reproach. So seldom had she turned her hostility on herself and allowed herself to indulge in self-pity. The infant had put in one last stand for vulnerability before the bitch consumed the spirit of the feminine aspect once more.

The woman waited. Time passed. All was quiet for too long.

She felt her irritation rise at the loathsome creature on earth to whom she was bound by this invisible cord.

The woman could not comprehend the man's passivity. It fueled her rage. His silence shattered her frame of mind and crumbled her foundation.

She had the sensation that the more she fought, the quieter and more limp he became.

She knew he did not sense her, and he was equally oblivious to her absence, but she took offense anyway. She took offense that he appeared to ignore her and that he appeared to ignore her out of spite. If he had been aware of her—or even felt her absence—then he would be ignoring her out of spite. And for that he should be punished.

What had he done to cause her to become a bitch? What had he done to exile her to the moon?

Yes, it was she who chose to go to the moon because it was the only place she could go where she could give her true nature free reign. But had not the man squeezed her nature and pinched it in just the right way to make her desperate enough to make such a dramatic exit?

The woman could not remember the details. She could not even critically assess the validity of her present feelings. It was what she felt in the moment, and it justified her bitter momentary feelings against her male aspect.

If only they would send another army against me, she thought. Let me fight a host of warriors rather than struggle against this thin thread of infinite strength that binds me to the insignificant organism.

What epic stories I could create if only others existed against whom I could compete and grow and adapt and finally learn to destroy, she thought further.

But this male aspect bound her to earth, and furthermore bound her to the moon. This attachment of male bonding was persistent, and—even worse—it was relentless.

The quiet, relentless bond was more irritating to her than the moon dust that got between her heels and her shoes. It was more irritating than moon dust, and it was more hostile than the most aggressive beasts they had sent after her. She had vanquished them all, but she could not vanquish this pathetic beast that did not even rise in her estimation to deserve being called pathetic.

Her mind was rambling, but she was unaware of it. She had to fight against something. Was it her mind she fought against, or this incessant connection to earth and the man?

The worm. Yes, the worm was what she wanted to destroy. The man was a worm.

The worm crawled across the surface of the moon. It was gray with moon dust.

Finally, they have sent a creature for me to destroy, she thought. It is so much better than feasting on my own mind.

And the woman rose and stepped on the worm. The worm turned against the woman's foot. It put up a brave fight as only a worm can.

The woman twisted her foot and mashed the worm deeper and deeper into the dust.

"You worm. You empty, worthless, gutless, squirming, writhing piece of slime," the woman said.

When the woman pulled away her foot, the two ends of the worm still wiggled, but the center of it was flattened and completely still.

Then the two active ends of the worm broke away from the dead, lifeless center, and each became a new worm.

"So they sent you to play games, did they?"

In unison the worms responded, "We come to kill you and eat you and learn to become the bitch of bitches."

The woman was about to step on one of the two worms according to her reactionary nature, but another reaction interrupted her before she could do it.

"What happens if I don't step on you? What happens if I don't play this game, and I keep you from multiplying?"

And the woman watched the worms squirm helplessly in the dust.

* * *

After he and himself had been quiet for an hour, the man spoke.

The man said, "If I let myself go completely, they would put me away. It would be nice to be put away for awhile, but they don't let you walk out of those closets simply when you feel like you feel better."

Himself was silent.

The man continued. "They missed their opportunity. There must have been a time—perhaps when I first fell off my horse—when I would have paid the hundred and fifty an hour for them to help me back on my horse."

Himself was still silent.

"Then the moment I became content to walk around on foot and merely pretend I was on my horse, they certainly had an opportunity to put me away, and I would have gone obediently and yielded to their treatment."

Silence.

"But now I've gone so long on foot, and I've made myself function as though I rode the same kind of horse as everyone else that there is little hope and even less of a point in trying to get back on my horse."

Silence.

"I have become my own horse, and I ride it better and more gallantly than anyone else rides their own common nags. I know how to keep a firm footing, and when I do stumble, I know how to regain my balance.

The man became concerned about himself's absence. He continued, but with an urgent voice as though to draw the attention of his absent self.

"I have a hard time to keep from mocking the others openly when they fall off their horses and think that the world is at an end. They do not know—and do not want to know—that they have much more stability on their own two feet than they have on any kind of horse they might find to ride. Did you say something?"

But himself had not said anything. The man was still talking into the darkness.

"I do not blame them, though. When the entire basis of human interaction, human culture, and human economy depends on trading and manufacturing and selling and marketing and repairing horses—new horses and old horses—it is rather quaint, if not absolutely crazy, to presume that one can get by without a horse. But how much better it is to create the illusion that you live according to these fundamental rules of the game while actually living beyond them in a transcendent state of self-fulfillment! And how much better yet to transcend the cynical grouch who complains endlessly about the worthlessness and emptiness and waste of modern society. Don't you agree?"

Silence.

"It's true that sometimes you have to go into the closet to get away, but then you also know when to let yourself out.

And then the man knew where himself had gone. Himself had gone into its own closet to get off the horse that the man was riding too hard.

The man smiled.

The man felt the silence all around him. He did not notice any longer when the blower of the furnace came on, so he did not feel his wallet draining its meager contents with each electrical surge. He did not feel the connectedness with the community that was bound together by the common electrical grid. He did not hear the cars out on the freeway—not even as white noise.

The man did not hear himself either. He did not hear himself because himself had gone into its own closet. The man hoped that himself had remembered to take a bucket or jar or some kind of container for liquid into the closet. He was confident that himself had learned his own lessons. Himself was sharp in that way.

The man was disconnected. He was disconnected in the way he had sought to be when he had conceived the idea to enter the closet.

The man had much confidence that he had discovered something new and important in his life. It was so new and so important that he would not be able to share it with anyone. They would not have the words for such a mode of being, and even if they did, they would probably be disturbing words like off-kilter, nuts, screw loose, mad, insane, crazy, lunatic.

They would not understand even with words like transcendent, enlightened, 'pataphysical, lofty, or sublime because they had butchered such terms with frivolous connotations and associations with banal experiences that belong to the realm of people who ride firmly on well-saddled horses.

He could set up a class to teach others how to disconnect by entering the closet, staying in the closet for a time, and then come out the other side, but few people would venture to take such a class. People simply like to ride horses, and those who ride horses do not like to feel their own feet on the ground.

And then too, would not people be at least confused, if not horrified, at what he would mean by coming out of the closet? It had a well-entrenched meaning that would completely obscure his point.

The man was so disconnected and in touch with his silence that he did not hear the knock, knock, knocking at his front door.

* * *

The man and the woman had returned to their boat, and in their boat, they had returned to the submarine.

"Why did they behave so strangely?" the tree asked the rock.

"It's how they reproduce," the rock said.

"I like how trees reproduce," the tree said.

The rock said nothing.

"How do rocks reproduce?" the tree asked.

"You don't want to know," the rock said grimly. "It's even more disgusting than how people do it."

The submarine sank beneath the surface of the ocean and left the tree and rock and island and the entire region of the North Pacific.

"You said they would return," the tree said to the rock.

"So I was wrong. I never claimed to know everything."

"You do know a lot, though. I think it's okay to be wrong sometimes."

"What do you know about being wrong?" The rock asked the tree, "You don't know enough to be wrong about anything."

"I'm sure you are right about that. It feels right anyway."

"You know all about feeling, don't you?"

"Sometimes I think that is all I know. But I know something else now too."

"What is this thing that you have come to know?" the rock asked.

"I know you were right the first time."

"Right about what?"

"The people coming back. See the people-whale has returned."

But the submarine had not returned. Another submarine had appeared.

"Now we are both wrong. Welcome to the club," the rock said. The rock had to squint in the sunshine that reflected off the cold, still water. Deep blue water. Deep green water, then deep blue again.

"So it is a real whale this time?" the tree asked hopefully.

"No, it is a different submarine from a different culture. See the different flag painted on the conning tower?"

"I can't see as clearly as you can. But I will believe you."

"You don't have to believe me, but it's true all the same."

A boat left the submarine and approached the shore with three men in it. Two men left the boat when it was close to shore. They had instruments with them similar to the instruments the people from the first submarine had brought with them.

The two men removed camping equipment from the boat.

When the boat was empty, the third man took the boat back to the submarine, and the submarine returned to the depths of the ocean.

"Why do these men speak funny?" the tree asked the rock.

"They speak a different language than the people who were here before."

The two men examined Morton with their instruments.

"Why are they so interested in Morton?"

The rock sighed. "They aren't interested in Morton. They are interested in the markings that the man and the woman made on old Mort."

"Morton doesn't like to be called Mort."

"Mort doesn't have to like it. Don't worry, buttercup, these men will discover soon enough that you are the only object of real interest around here. The others were just throwing off any pursuers by marking up Morton instead of you."

"Why am I so special?"

"Wouldn't we all like to know? Then we could bottle it up and sell it to all the tourists who will certainly swarm this nameless, graceless island."

"I'd like to see more people come to the island. These people fascinate me."

"I'm not surprised."

"Maybe then the island would get a proper name and not be just a nameless godforsaken pile of rocks as you call it.

"What's so important about having a name?"

"It's not the name that would be important: the important thing would be to not be forsaken by God anymore."

"It's just a figure of speech, I told you before."

"Then at least we would not be forsaken by people anymore."

"Be careful what you wish for."

The two men lost interest in Morton and turned their attention and their instruments on other nearby trees.

"They are looking for you, whale child."

"I'm here," the tree shouted the best it could in a voice imitating the language of the two men.

The two men turned their instruments on the tree and became excited. They examined the tree thoroughly, particularly the markings that the previous party had left from their instruments when they had examined the tree.

The two men recorded everything and took many pictures.

When night fell, the men stopped their work and relaxed in the same way the man and the woman from the previous party had relaxed.

"Why do these people like to try to reproduce themselves after examining me?"

"They aren't trying to reproduce themselves," the rock said.

"What are they doing?"

"They are making rocks."

Part II

Chapter 7

The knocking on the man's front door grew louder, but still he did not hear it. Perhaps he heard it in the same way that he still heard the furnace blower and the cars on the freeway. Perhaps he heard it all but tuned it all out in the suspension of awareness he had achieved. The suspension of awareness that disconnected him entirely from the world except for one thin strand that connected him to existence: his patient anticipation of the sound of the alarm clock that would rouse him from his slumber and his stupor at the usual time.

The man did not hear the fine tools gently picking the lock of his front door. His ears were highly attenuated and would have been sensitive to such delicate sounds if he had the mind to pay attention to such things rather than only paying attention to the silence that existed everywhere between the sounds.

Had the man been aware of the sounds of the fine tools gently picking the lock of his front door, he would have appreciated that the agents came to him so carefully rather than bursting down the door so obtusely and thrashing his home in search of any shred of evidence they could use against him—all the while destroying every shred of evidence in their belligerent and excitable earnestness. He would have appreciated their careful approach if he had been aware of their approach at all. But he was not aware.

The woman entered first, followed by a man, but not the man she had tried to reproduce with by the tree on the island before she and he had returned by boat to the submarine.

The man was followed by other men. But none of the men who entered the man's house had been with the woman on the island in the North Pacific or on the submarine that the tree had mistaken for a whale.

The men followed the woman's orders very carefully. They let her roam freely while they analyzed the man's house with their instruments. The men were in constant communication with the observers at headquarters. Some of the observers had been on the submarine with the woman, and fewer had been on the island. None of the observers had been the man with whom the woman had tried to reproduce by the tree on the island. That man was busy doing other things.

The woman left the men to do their analysis as they had been trained. She examined the man's house as she had been trained.

She entered the man's bedroom and asked the technicians to leave her alone in the room.

The men left and did their work in other parts of the man's house. They paid careful attention to the new quilt that adorned the man's sofa.

The woman turned off the light and breathed deeply. She turned on the light again and looked under the man's bed.

Nothing.

She rummaged through the drawers of his dresser but found nothing of interest.

She examined the contents of his desk and file cabinet. He was as dull as she had anticipated.

The woman hesitated at the door of the man's closet. Then she opened it.

The man fluttered his eyes at the suddenly bright light shining on him, but he did not waken. The woman missed this reaction by the man because she did not notice him at first.

The first thing the woman noticed was the damp blanket dripping liquid down the wall of the closet. Only after her eyes followed the drips to the floor did she see a pair of feet with ten toes and at the other end of the closet floor a head with wide, moist eyes that stared far into the distance, the pupils now dilating now shrinking at random intervals and with random intensity.

The woman said the man's name, but he did not respond.

The woman removed the wet blanket from the shelf above the shirts. She left the bedroom and found the man's laundry room. She put the blanket in his wash machine.

On her way back from the laundry room, she asked the technicians if they had found anything.

They told her the only anomalies came from the bedroom.

She told them to keep at it, and she returned to the bedroom. She turned off the light and instructed the men not to enter.

The woman knew her way around the room in the darkness. She opened the door to the closet and said the man's name again.

The man did not answer her, but his hand took hold of her calf.

The woman asked the man what he wanted.

The man did not speak, but he pulled the woman's leg as though trying to pull her into the closet.

The woman said there was not enough room.

The man sat up and crossed his legs. He pulled the woman into the closet, and she could feel the position he sat in, and she could feel that he wanted her to sit on the floor of the closet next to him. And she did. And she was thankful he had given her the dry side.

* * *

The woman on the moon was still on the moon, and she was still a woman and she was still connected to the slut man who now sat in the closet with another woman.

The woman on the moon was still a bitch. She was still as much of a bitch as she had ever been. She was still as much of a bitch as the moon had ever seen, but from the earth's perspective, she was the inheritor of a long line of bitches that the earth had produced in the many long years and centuries and millennia that it had harbored such predators within its warm confines.

The woman was still a bitch, but she had made a fatal mistake, and she would never be more of a bitch than she had been at the moment she had made the mistake, and she would find her bitch fade until she was no more or less a bitch than the female aspect of any being on the earth or the moon.

She had paused with curiosity and perspective in her attack on the worm after it had divided into two worms. She had yielded to the irony of a situation rather than blunder ahead with the full aggressive force of her nature.

It had only been a pause, and in the next moment she attacked the worm with full vigor. But despite her commitment to defeating it in the most merciless manner, the pause had given her enemies a foothold from which they would win the war.

In the instant that the woman had decided to confound their expectations by not attacking when she normally would, the two worms grew heavy armor.

As the woman renewed her attack on them, fueled by regret now in addition to her over-heated bitchiness, their armor grew stronger, and the two worms then began to grow larger and longer under her furious assault.

When the woman noticed that her feet no longer were as effective against the worm, she sought to end things then and there with her mouth.

The woman devoured the two worms as swiftly and as completely as she had devoured all the beings they had sent against her since the offensive had begun.

Three days passed, and all was fine.

The woman prowled the moon alone as she had done previously, contriving ways to free herself from the tether that connected her to earth. She dreamed of Mars, Jupiter, and Saturn. She dreamed of devouring the entire solar system and after that the galaxy.

But three days later, the woman found that while she had devoured the worms completely, she had not absorbed them completely. What was left of them had combined into a single capsule, and she defecated it in her rarely used waste shelter. Much time had passed since she had needed the waste shelter because she had learned to transform everything she ate entirely into herself.

The woman did not examine the waste closely. That was her second mistake, although there was little she could have done to stop the string of cause and effect that had already been put in motion. While her first mistake had made every-thing that followed inevitable, her second mistake increased the pace at which the inevitable happened.

The capsule followed the woman out of the waste shelter, and it shot into the sky where it orbited the moon high above. The woman was unable to reach it, and the capsule grew and gained strength.

The woman only noticed the new object in the black sky above her after it had grown large enough to contain a human being, and at that point, it did contain a human being: al-though, whether the human had been a part of the worm from the beginning or had entered the capsule only when it was large enough to contain a human is open to interpreta-tion, speculation, and imagination.

What is not open to interpretation, speculation, or imagi-nation is that the woman recognized the capsule for what it was and what it had been. She recognized that all creatures that had invaded her moon and her space and her being be-fore the worm showed up had indeed been her own invention to keep herself from getting bored and to exercise her bitch.

But this worm had been sent by someone else. This worm had been a trick, and the woman had tricked herself into fal-ling for the trick at the precise moment that it mattered most for her to act boldly to keep hold of her crown of queen bitch of the moon.

The woman had not created the worm, and that was why she had not been able to absorb it entirely. That was why she had been unable to absorb the essential aspect of the worm that now flew high above her with a human being inside it. And it was not just any human being.

Inside the capsule that drifted high above the barking mad bitch of the moon was the man that had tried to reproduce with the woman near the tree on the island in the North Pacific.

The man in the capsule was adjusting to his new configuration and working up his courage to do what he had been sent to do for the good of the woman on the moon, the good of the man on the floor of the closet, and the good of all human kind. He had no idea that it was also for the good of all treekind, but it was just as well: that would have put him under too much pressure.

* * *

"I think you are kidding me," said the tree.

"I am not," said the rock.

"How can rocks come from people? People should come from people and rocks from rocks."

"Yet you think a tree like yourself comes from a whale."

"I understand how a seed can pass through a whale. But you don't understand the spiritual part of such an experience," the tree said.

"You are crazy," said the rock.

"No more crazy than saying that rocks come from people. You can't even explain how it happens, much less show the spiritual side."

"The mechanical process is easy to explain. Two men try to reproduce, and one man conceives a rock in his womb. The humans call it a kidney. Then after various periods of gestation—it depends on the type of rock being formed—it passes out the man's urinary tract and into the light of the world."

"These men seem to like making rocks."

"Some men like to make rocks, some like to make little people, and some like to make both."

"Do any like to make trees?"

"No. If they make trees, they do it as whales do it: without any awareness at all that they do it."

"You told me that rocks existed before people ever did."

"That's right."

"Then how were rocks made before people arrived?"

"Oh, any pair of male mammals can make a rock."

"Aren't whales mammals?"

"Yes, they are. And big ones too. But the biggest rocks do not come from the biggest mammals. The big mammals make many small rocks."

"So we could be brothers?"

"No."

"We could not have come from the same whale?"

"We are neither male nor female, so we can't be brother or sister. And I am much too old to have passed through the same living mammal as you did."

"So some mammals existed before rocks?"

"No. Rocks existed before mammals and trees and every other living thing."

"Then how—"

"Shut up, would you?"

"I'm just trying to—"

"Never mind what you are trying to do. Just stop with all the questions."

"Now you have become grouchy again."

"It's hard not to be grouchy with you around."

"You were fine when that woman was here."

"I was in love."

"Can't you love one of these men? I like the one that tries to give the rocks to the other."

"These men make me nervous," the rock said. "I don't like them."

"You don't like them because they are not women?"

"I don't like them because they are not here for any good purpose."

"You don't like that they have come to make rocks?"

"That's not their primary purpose."

"Then why are they here?"

"I don't know, but it has something to do with those people who were here first, and it has something to do with you and all the instruments they use on you."

"Do you think the woman will return?"

"I hope so."

"What happens when two female mammals try to reproduce themselves? What do they make?"

"They make pure love."

"Wow. Really?"

"No. But they think they do, and that's all that matters to female mammals—particularly females of the human species."

"So what do they make?"

"Trouble."

"You said that's what they make for males of the species when they don't make babies."

"Okay, then two females don't make trouble when they try to reproduce themselves."

"Then what do they make?"

"Use your imagination. What do you think they make?"

"Are you telling me you don't know?"

"I'm telling you to use your own imagination sometimes instead of badgering me for answers."

"You don't know, do you? You don't know like you really don't know where rocks and trees come from, but you have used your imagination to create possible answers—at least possible enough that a silly tree like me might believe."

"Don't get so sensitive. I'm trying to protect you."

"Protect me from what?"

"The truth."

"The truth about what?"

The tree leaned closer to the rock. It wanted to lean all the way over to the surface of the high tide so it could hear the rock whisper its truth. But the tree only swayed slightly in the still air as though a breeze blew across the ocean and the island.

"The truth about nothing," the rock said.

"Nothing? What about nothing?"

"You are not yet old enough to understand."

"Understand nothing?"

"Yeah, nothing. Nothing as something."

"If it's something then it can't be nothing."

"As I said, you can't understand."

"So you are saying that when two female people try to reproduce themselves they make nothing?"

"No. I'm not saying that at all."

"Then what are you saying?"

"I'm saying I don't know anything about it. I know nothing. Nothing at all. Just as you said."

Chapter 8

The woman in the closet looked at the man in the closet. The woman looked at the man, but she could not see the man. She could not see the man because it was too dark in the closet to see anything.

The woman waited for her eyes to adjust to the darkness so she could perhaps see the man even a little. But it was too dark in the closet for the woman to see the man even a little— even after her eyes had adjusted.

The woman did not see the man, but she could feel him. She could feel his presence, and she could feel and hear his breathing.

The woman could not feel the man's body even though she sat close to him on the floor of his small closet. The man pushed her hand away from him each time she tried to touch him. He did not speak to her, and he pushed her away, carefully delineating his half of the closet floor.

The man began to shake. The woman could not see the man shake, but she could hear it, and she could feel it. She tried to touch him, but he pushed her away again. She tried to wrap the blanket around him more snuggly, but he pushed her away again.

The man's shaking turned into more violent nervous convulsions. The woman tried to feel what the man was experiencing, but she could feel nothing beyond the physical convulsions.

The woman spoke the man's name, but the man did not reply.

The woman opened the closet door and started to crawl into the room. She did not know if she was leaving to get help or just leaving to leave the man alone. She was not sure what he needed. She was not sure what he wanted. She was not even sure what she wanted. She was rarely so unsure about what to do.

She was rarely so unsure about what to do, and that is why she allowed herself to return to the floor of the closet when the man grabbed her arm and drew her back inside. He shut the door softly.

"What do you want? Where are you?" the woman asked the darkness.

The man was too far away to hear her. He continued shaking, and he continued to refuse her attempts to calm him by her touch. Only when his convulsions grew so strong that he began to bang his head against the wall of the closet did he allow her to touch him. He allowed her to place her hand between his head and the wall to keep his head from hitting the bare sheetrock.

The woman began to speak again, but the man clasped his hand over her mouth. He held it firmly. In such a vulnerable position, the woman began to fear the man's physical strength, but the man did nothing more than gently cover her mouth with his hand.

The woman touched the man's hand that covered her mouth. She touched it softly. She touched it gently. The man's tremors began to subside. He stopped banging his head against her hand on the wall.

The man removed his hand from the woman's mouth. He wrapped himself in the blanket more securely. His shaking slackened until he was merely swing back and forth then forward and backward, but not as violently as before, and not enough to require her physical intervention as before.

The man even hummed a little, but he did not speak. He did not speak, and he covered the woman's mouth again when she began to hum along with him.

The man refused to let the woman speak. He refused to let her touch him, and he refused to let her leave the closet. But the woman did not feel trapped. She knew she could leave at any moment, but he did not want her to leave, so she stayed. She stayed to try to understand what was going on with the man.

She could not understand what was going on with the man because she had never needed to go into the closet herself. She had never needed to disconnect in the way that the man had invented for him and himself to disconnect.

But just as the sea below the surface is calm even in the most violent of storms, the man maintained his sense of peace throughout the ordeal. Indeed the man was still oblivious to the woman's presence. He was oblivious to her voice, her touch, and her invitations. He was oblivious to the men who scoured his house with their instruments looking for all the things the observers had sent them to find.

The man was oblivious to the observers, and he was oblivious to the tree in the distant North Pacific, and he was oblivious to the woman on the more distant moon who felt the connection to him so strongly.

The only thing that kept the man from completely detaching himself from space and time and humanity was the vigilant sentry he had left behind to listen for the alarm clock.

The woman felt the man calm down. The woman had no idea what to do with a man who sat so resolutely on the floor of his closet.

The woman tried to leave the closet again, and this time the man let her. She left the closet and gathered the men who were examining the man's house.

The woman told the men they could leave the house and they should stay alert in case she needed them.

The men left the house.

The woman made a full report to the observers and then signed off. The woman lay down on the man's sofa and pulled the new quilt over her, but she sensed something was missing.

What she did not know was that she had left herself in the man's closet.

* * *

A heavy wind swept over the island in the North Pacific. A cold wind blew through the trees on the island, the nameless godforsaken island in the North Pacific.

And Morton died.

The old birch tree that had lived for many and many years among the firs of the island died when the cold wind swept over the island.

Morton did not die from the mutilation and vandalism that the man and the woman had performed on it. Morton did not die of jealousy over the attention that the tree by the shore received—the tree by the rock that was so singular and yet still so much like a tree.

Morton simply died from old age. But Morton did not die alone. That is not to say that Morton did not die without other trees around it. Most trees die with other trees around it. What it means to say that Morton did not die alone is that Morton was not the only living being who died when Morton died.

Sometimes when a tree dies, it dies standing up, and it remains standing for many years, and perhaps it even decomposes entirely on its feet, as it were.

But at other times, a tree falls when it dies.

Morton's death was of this second kind. Morton fell over.

And as Morton's main trunk (for a birch can have several trunks) and all the branches attached to that trunk came crashing to the ground in the frigid wind, it crashed across the tent in which the two men slept. The two men who had been left by the submarine to examine the tree and who had later tried to make rocks.

The man who had conceived the rocks in his womb died when Morton fell on him. The other man—the man whom the tree had begun to like—was largely spared. He had a few cuts and bruises, but the worst injury was to his soul.

The trees and rocks of the island were inconsolable over Morton's demise. At first they were unaware that Morton had not died alone. They were as reactionary as all living things are, and they blamed his death on the frivolous and petulant people who had scarred Morton so badly.

But when the living man cried from his soul, the trees and rocks of the island, and the wind—the wind too— sympathized and forgot the accusations they had mustered against humankind.

The rock, however, was unmoved. The rock had seen many deaths in its time, and neither Morton's death nor the man's death touched it.

The tree wept. The tree felt its sap fall and drain out through its roots.

"What will we do without Morton?" the tree asked the rock through its sobs.

"Life goes on, so to speak," the rock said.

The surviving man pulled the remains of Morton off the remains of the dead man. The man cleared the tent of death and destruction, and he took inventory of what remained. He tried to communicate with his observers, but the radio was either dead or in too much grief to work properly.

"I think I love him even more now," the tree told the rock.

"Don't get too attached," the rock said.

The man carried the radio to a clearing and tried to reach his observers. But the radio did not work.

The man stepped through the mid-tide and onto the rock. The radio began to make garbled noises as it recovered from its sorrow.

And the rock turned over.

The rock. The rock that had remained in place through tide and gale. Through sunshine and moonshine. Through star-shine. The rock that knew everything, and what it did not know it would use its imagination to create a knowledge that was truer than true. This rock had rolled over at the touch of this man and his radio.

And the man fell.

At first the tree thought the man had died. The radio had certainly died. It drifted on the waning tide far out to sea where perhaps it would one day wash up on the shores of

Minami Tori Shima and sprout a radio tree. But the man did not die. The man only lost consciousness in the shallow water—too shallow to drown in the shallow and grieving waves.

The tree asked the rock why it had made such a thing happen.

The rock was silent.

The tree was empty. The tree was empty and sad and as sad as it had ever been in its short life.

When the man regained consciousness, the tree became happy—although happy within the general feeling of sadness.

The man rose from the water, but only on his hands and knees. He could not stand. He could not stand because his leg was broken.

The rock had killed the radio and broken the man's leg. And the tree was sad about death. The deaths of Morton and the other man and the radio and the man's broken leg. But the tree was happy that the man was not dead.

The strangest of the strong feelings the tree felt at that moment was a new feeling. A feeling of utter shame for the behavior of the rock.

"You did that on purpose," the tree shouted over the wind.

"I cannot hear you," the rock said.

"Why don't you roll away from me and from the other trees and from this island forever?"

"I'm not going anywhere," the rock declared.

The man pulled himself up the shore, and he leaned against the tree.

The tree wanted to wrap its branches around the man and comfort him until he was healed.

The man moved to the side of the tree away from the shore, away from the homicidal rock, and away from the cold wind.

The tree felt its sap rising once more. It became warm from within and wanted to share its warmth with the broken man who sought shelter at its roots.

* * *

The man in the capsule looked down on the woman on the moon.

The woman on the moon looked up at the capsule above her that contained the man, though at this time she did not know it contained the man. She did know, however, that the capsule had grown from the worm she had failed to destroy. But maintaining her consistency, she refused to accept that she had failed to destroy it. Instead, she became incensed that it had failed to die. And she wanted to kill it all the more, and she wanted it to live all the more so she could kill it again and again and yet again.

The man prepared to make his move. He maneuvered his capsule into a gradual descent, but he pulled back when he saw that the woman was not alone.

The woman had summoned first one then two then three partners. Three partners, then six.

The man knew he would need reinforcements. He contacted his observers and made his report and asked for reinforcements.

The observers thanked him for his report, but they refused his request for reinforcements.

The man said he was running out of fuel and that he stood no chance against the army that was forming against him.

The observers said on the contrary, he stood no chance against the woman while she was alone, but he had a moderate chance now that the woman's resources were divided.

The man sighed and accepted his fate.

The man sat the capsule down in a distant crater. He exited the capsule and climbed to the crest of the crater. The sun was directly overhead. He had no shadow, and the crater cast no shadow.

Twelve figures escorted the regal thirteenth figure into the crater.

The man retreated to a boulder deep within the crater, and he waited. He did not cast a shadow, and he felt more secure where he was than any other place he could have been on the moon.

He had a good vantage point. He could see without being seen. What he saw was twenty-five women enter the crater opposite him. The one in the rear was the one he was most interested in.

The first twenty-four women spread out and circled the bottom of the crater, slowly making their way toward him.

The twenty-fifth woman—the woman of the moon—went directly to the capsule and searched it. She wanted to eat it, but she knew what had happened before, and she was not about to mess around with such a thing making its way through her guts again. No telling what would come out the other side.

Then the man was confused when the ring of women entirely avoided the boulder he was behind, and instead they closed the circle at the bottom of the crater just below him.

The man was even more confused when he noticed that the two clones that had closed the circle as the leaders of the left and right flanks held between them a man who looked much like himself.

The twenty-four women circled the man and in one voice they called the woman who was drooling over the capsule.

The woman approached the gathering.

"You have found him?"

"As you see."

"Where?"

"The women pointed to the boulder that the man still hid behind.

The woman approached the boulder, but the ring of women intervened.

"Here is your man," the women said to the woman.

"This is a clone you have created to trick me. You have betrayed me," the woman said. She grabbed the woman nearest her and tore off her head.

The ring of women drew tighter together. The man noticed there were only twelve women in the ring surrounding the man's clone.

"We assure you, mistress, we found this pathetic creature, this most pathetic of all creatures, hiding behind that boulder."

The woman took another woman by the hair and dragged her to the ground. She forced her to eat the body of the decapitated woman.

The woman gagged and choked and cried, but in the end, she did what the woman commanded.

The woman stood the woman up.

"Now create a man for me," she demanded. "Create a man for me like you did when I wasn't watching."

The other five women still surrounded the first man they had created. The woman thought about what her mistress had ordered, and strengthened by her recent feeding, she succeeded in creating another man on her own.

The new man stepped out of the capsule.

The woman devoured the woman who had just created the new man. She belched and two swords came out of her mouth. She gave one to each of the male clones.

"You will fight to the death. The loser will be our dessert, and the winner will have the honor of hunting the man we truly seek."

The first of the cloned men did not know what to do. The second one did. He thrust this sword through the heart of the first man, and then stood in silence as the six remaining women had their dessert.

When they had nearly finished with the man, the man with the sword cut the head off the nearest woman. The other five women began to eat the woman.

In this manner, the man killed off all the cloned women until he alone stood before the pale bitch goddess of the moon. He called out to the man behind the boulder that he could show himself.

"Your reinforcement has arrived."

Chapter 9

Maybe it was the smell of death. The smell of death borne on the wind through the trees. A tree, a man, a radio. Dead.

The grizzly came slowly, alertly, but with a certainty beyond mere curiosity. The grizzly came down the path along the shore. The grizzly bear came down the path that cut the tree off from the rest of the forest.

The tree felt the bear coming long before the man with the broken leg felt the bear coming. The tree tried to warn the man, but the man did not understand any of the tree's words or gestures. The man was in shock, and he had little awareness of the finer details of his environment like the tree trying to warn him that a bear was approaching.

The rock could sense the bear's presence.

"Lolly bear will finish what I started," said the rock.

"Lolly? That bear is not named Lolly," the tree said, openly defying the rock's knowledge.

"Ask her."

The tree shook itself as hard as it could in a final effort to alert the man of the coming danger.

The man did not feel the tree shake, or if he did, he did not correctly interpret its message. But the man did hear the snapping of twigs, and a moment later he heard the grunt that shocked him out of his shock.

The man crawled across the path and slid up against a larger tree with a dense patch of undergrowth at the base, and he hid behind it.

The grizzly bear stepped into view and sniffed the air. The grizzly bear was a large gray female.

The tree felt its bark tighten in anticipation of the bear's sharp claws.

The bear lumbered over to the tent and sniffed at the dead man. It pawed at the dead man and hit him in the head a few times to make sure he was really dead and not just playing dead.

The dead man was really dead.

Then the bear turned its attention to Morton who was lying across the tent and across the path to the edge of the shore where its smallest, highest branches dipped now and then in the waves. Many things were new by the shore on this day, thought the bear.

The bear tried to break open Morton in search of grubs, but the tree had not been lying on the ground long enough to have the moisture and its attendant environment develop into a bear's pantry.

The grizzly worked its way down the tree to its trunk and found the fertile ground where the root system had been torn up. The moisture and its attendant environment under Morton's roots had developed into a bear's pantry, and that had done much to shorten Morton's days.

The bear had its feast.

The tree and the man waited anxiously as the bear took its time to savor every morsel of fat and protein it could get its tongue and claws and teeth into.

When the bear had finished eating, it scanned the downed tree once more. It noticed the strange marks that the man and the woman had embedded in Morton's bark. It did not know what the marks meant.

The bear tried to claw its own marks into Morton's dead bark, but Morton only bounced up and down. The bear preferred to claw the bark of a standing tree.

So the bear approached the tree and proceeded to do the things to it that the tree was not sure were pleasurable or painful, but perhaps were both.

"Are you blind, Lolly?" the rock shouted.

The bear clawed deeply into the tree as high as it could reach. The tree was young enough that the bear could make the tree sway far and wide when it reached so high and clawed so deeply.

"Lolly!"

The bear looked at the tree.

"I didn't say anything," the tree said.

The bear grunted.

"There's a man behind the tree just down the path," the rock said. "He is only playing dead, but he will likely be dead soon enough whether you have anything to do about it or not."

The tree was annoyed at the rock for giving such information to the bear.

The bear looked down the path to the tree that had the dense patch of undergrowth at its base.

"Yeah, that one," the rock said.

The tree did its best to intercede.

"The rock says when female mammals try to reproduce with other females, they think they make pure love but they really only make trouble."

The bear looked at the tree.

"I said I didn't know," the rock said defensively.

"The rock said it with much confidence," the tree said.

"Lolly can clarify it for us, right Lolly?" the rock said.

The bear looked at the tree and then at the rock and then back at the tree.

"Why do you care?" the bear growled.

"Just answer the question, would ya?" the rock said.

The bear waded out through the shallow high tide and pushed the rock over and over out into the deeper parts of the shoreline. The bear pushed the rock under water until it fell into a pit. The last roll nearly pulled the bear into the watery pit too because as the rock dropped it formed a drag behind it, and a wave crashed over the bear. The bear fought the force of the wave above and the drag of the falling rock beneath.

But the bear recovered and swam strongly until it reached solid footing. It ambled back to the path and entered the forest, completely ignoring—or perhaps forgetting—the man who was playing dead.

* * *

The man in the closet was deep in his disconnected, far-off place. He was deep, and he was disconnected, and he was far-off.

It had been dark and silent and quiet and dark. It had been particularly silent since himself had retreated to himself's own closet.

That was why he was surprised when he heard the soft, sweet voice, and he was twice surprised that the soft, sweet voice was a female voice.

"I did not know I could speak to myself in a female voice," the man said.

"I am not your voice," herself said.

"Where did you come from?"

"From her."

"When?"

"Some time ago. I don't know how long ago exactly."

The man thought for some time. He was not sure if he was speaking his lines out loud or thinking them.

"You must be thinking them," herself said.

"You can read my mind?"

"Not completely. I pick up on a few phrases here and there."

"But when I speak—or think—to you directly?"

"Yes, I understand every word you intend for me."

"How did you get here?"

A long silence held the man's attention. He began to wonder if herself had dissipated.

"Hello?" the man said.

"I'm here. I'm just thinking how to answer your question."

"Is it so difficult to know?"

"It is more interesting to tell how I got out."

"Out of her? Who is her?"

"You had a visitor while you were disconnected. She sat with you for a time, and then she left."

"Did I make a fool of myself?"

"No, but *you* would think you did."

"Who is she?"

"She is her, and I am herself."

"And she left you behind to reach me?"

"No. She would never detach herself from her willingly. I enjoyed the time she spent in here, and I decided to stay."

"What did she want with me?"

"You will have to let her tell you that. You can ask her when you wake up."

The blower of the furnace turned on. The man did not notice it, but herself did.

Herself had to shout to be heard, "What is that noise?"

"Nothing. You will get used to it."

Herself told the man that she did not hear him because the noise was too loud. The man remained silent until the blower turned off again.

"How can you stand that noise?" she asked.

"I learned to talk over it and listen through it."

"And whom do you talk to?"

"Before, I talked to himself. Now, I talk to you."

"Where is himself?"

"He found his own closet to disconnect in. Disconnect from my talking. So after you disconnected from her, how did you find me? How did you get inside?

The voice was silent for a long time again, but the man was patient. He knew she had not gone anywhere.

"You are still connected to the alarm clock. I felt that connection and wiggled my way inside. Like a little mouse."

"I hope there's enough room for you," he said. "There should be since himself has gone into his own closet."

"There's more room than you know."

"What do you mean?"

"It is particularly empty in here."

"Come now, I know I have an above-average intelligence. I can't be that empty."

"I'm not in your head, silly. I'm in your heart."

The man tried to feel very deeply. He tried to feel for where herself was, but he could not feel her. He could only hear her—or perhaps think her; he was not sure which.

"Am I intruding?" herself asked the man. "She sleeps on your couch. I could return to her if you are uncomfortable with me being here."

"I want you to tell me more about this emptiness. I have never felt particularly empty."

"That's exactly it. You don't know what it is like to feel full, so of course you don't feel the emptiness. You feel the emptiness as normal."

"I have earnestly searched for love. It's not my fault I have never found anyone suitable."

"This isn't about love or finding a partner to love you. This is a deficiency in you. You are missing two key aspects of your life. You are only one-third of a full being.

"What will you charge me for this nonsense? I am already in debt beyond my means. I can't afford to give you anything for what you are trying to do."

"I'm just exploring on my own. I'm observing and reporting what I observe. I learned that from her."

"So how am I to fix this deficiency? You have the solution for sale in three easy installments, right?"

"I don't know what you can do. Maybe it has something to do with why she has come for you. I would recommend you listen to her and follow her advice. She's very good."

Himself came out of his closet.

"I thought I heard voices," himself said, "and I know I'm not crazy."

"A female voice at that!" he exclaimed. "I bet you didn't think we could pull it off, did you?" he asked himself.

"I did a convincing imitation of your mother earlier," himself said.

"I will let you boys talk," herself said. "I'm tired. We will speak again in the morning." And herself was gone.

The man and himself fell asleep and forgot all about herself.

* * *

The woman on the moon ate the man's reinforcement. The woman on the moon ate the reinforcement slowly. The reinforcement had yielded to this necessity. It was his duty as a reinforcement to sacrifice his existence for the success of the mission.

And yet this reinforcement had not been sent by the observers. This reinforcement had been materialized by the platoon of women that the woman had materialized to help her catch the man in the capsule.

The women had betrayed the woman from their own nature. But the man in the capsule had longed for a reinforcement, and his longing had penetrated the reinforcement's psyche and informed it of the mission at hand.

The woman savored every bite. The woman knew she was losing her powers, and she suspected she would not be able to materialize another such specimen. She knew she had something special in this one to enjoy.

When the man from the capsule approached the woman, she turned on him like a lion protecting its kill. So he gave her space.

The reinforcement chatted with the man during most of the process. The woman took her time, and the reinforcement had much to say, but none of it was very important. He was, after all, the product of women.

The man tried to carry his half of the conversation, but the reinforcement had too much to say. So the man listened. He listened from a distance. A safe distance.

The conversation ended when the woman ate the reinforcement's head.

The woman swallowed both swords, and at that point, the man and the woman were alone. No materialized phantasms or conjured cohorts to muddle the situation.

The woman tried to materialize another woman, but the figure appeared with only its torso and head, then it faded, and then it disappeared altogether.

"I won't give up," the woman said.

"I have no doubt," the man said.

The man was smaller than the woman. He attributed this to her long sojourn on the moon. The woman had inflated in the lower gravity of the moon.

The man and the woman looked at each other across the distance that separated them.

"What have you done to me?" the woman asked.

The man knew better than to argue with a bitch. He just stared at her.

"Why can't I materialize anything anymore?"

The man approached the woman and put his fingers to her mouth.

"Bite," he said.

She did, but she could not penetrate his skin with her teeth. She bit as hard as she could, but his skin was impervious to her gluttony.

The woman ran away from the man and hid in her sleeping shelter.

The man watched the woman run away. "Either fighting or running, isn't that just how it goes," the man said to himself.

The man trudged after the woman.

The woman watched the man approach her sleeping shelter. She locked the entrance and barricaded the windows. It was dark inside. She thought about the man. She thought about the man in the closet. The man she was attached to, locked to, and cursed to be connected to forever. She was behaving like the man. She was making her own closet and hiding in it.

Her behavior infuriated her. Her rage rose once more as it always had. She wanted to be full of angry, evil, and wicked imperatives when the man from the capsule arrived, and she would unleash the bitch of all bitches on him and annihilate him for all eternity.

But the man did not enter the woman's sleeping shelter. He waited outside in the balmy sunshine. He waited, anticipating the storm that brewed within. He suspected it might dissipate on its own if left enclosed long enough.

He was partially right.

Instead of blowing itself out, the storm found another outlet.

The woman could not stand the silence and the confines of her sleeping quarters, but she also suspected she was not yet furious enough to stand a chance against the man. So she fled out the rear of the sleeping shelter and ran across the crater, out into the plain of the moon, then into another crater. She felt her fury grow in the open expanse of space.

The man plodded after her on foot.

The woman wondered why the man did not chase her in his capsule; it would have been much faster. She hated the waiting.

The man stepped closer.

The angry bitch rose out of the crater and ran further away. She knew exactly what it would take to recover her invincibility.

The woman ran to the edge of the horizon. She had not seen the earth for as long as she could remember. She paused at the bottom of the last crater. The last crater before she would begin to see the earth. Once she saw the earth, her bitch would certainly increase to new proportions, and she would then be strong enough to take on the man from the capsule. She could feel the earth's pending presence by the tension in her connection to the useless slut man hiding in his closet below.

She always thought of the man as below her, and it was— as long as the connection went through the moon itself. She always felt the tension through her feet. But when she rose out of the crater and saw the stupid blue and white ball hanging just over the horizon, the tension was no longer buffered by the material moon; instead, the connection was free of the lunar substance, and the connection pulled the woman off her feet and dragged her on her back across the plains of the near side of the moon. Her body left a deep trench in the dust.

Chapter 10

The tree called out to the man that the grizzly bear was gone and that it was safe for him to come out from behind the other tree.

What the tree really wanted was for the broken man to crawl back across the path and take shelter against it once more. It wanted to feel the man whom it was beginning to love. It wanted to feel the man against the base of its trunk where he had been before the bear had appeared.

The man did not answer the tree. But the man did pull himself out from behind the undergrowth. He had guessed that it was safe to leave his hiding place, and he was hungry and thirsty, but mostly thirsty.

The man dragged himself across the path to the remains of the campsite. He knew his leg was broken, but he did not know what to do about it.

The bear had punctured the water container and had lapped up most of the water within. The man lapped up the rest of the water. He was still thirsty, but not as thirsty as before.

He looked through the first aid kit and found a packet of pain relievers. He wished the other man had not drunk the last of the vodka before they had gone to sleep the night before.

The man swallowed the pain relievers without aid of liquid. They had a sour, chalky taste going down, and he had little hope they would do much good for his pain.

The man found the tin of fish and opened it. The bear had not cleaned him out completely. He ate the fish and drank the oil in the bottom of the can.

The man would take care of the other man later. He did not know what he could do to bury his friend, but he wanted to do something. He did not know when the submarine would return. The ground station was waiting for his radio signal, but the radio was dead.

The man left the other man in the sleeping bag in the tent, and he dragged himself and his own sleeping bag across the path and to the tree. The tree that stood alone between the path and the water and now stood completely alone with the rock at the bottom of the ocean.

The man did not know why he was returning to that tree. He would have been safer behind the other tree. Safer from bears anyway. He would have been sheltered from the weather better behind any of the clusters of trees on the opposite side of the path from the tree.

Subconsciously, though, the man had felt warmth from that tree. Its warmth had been comforting, and even with his sleeping bag and any kind of a large fire he could make, the warmth of another living being was what he wanted most.

Consciously, he told himself that he wanted to return to that tree because he would have a good view of both the sea—in case of a rescue ship—and the inland part of the island—to see the approach of other bears.

A bear was just the sort of warm being he wanted to cuddle up to, but the claws and teeth and bad intentions would have come between them. So the man contented himself against the tree. He got himself into the sleeping bag and sat up against the tree with a minimum of pain in his leg.

And the tree began to glow. The other trees could not see the glow, but the man could feel it. At first he thought it was his body warmth getting trapped in the sleeping bag, but then it persisted despite the wind that blew into the sleeping bag from time to time. And it increased in warmth, and it increased in comfort.

The man put his neck against the tree, and then he put his hand against the tree. He turned around to make sure the tree was not on fire.

It was not.

The tree was happy, and the tree tried to comfort the man the best it could. The tree tried to speak to the man, but the tree could not speak the man's language, and the man could not have known how to interpret the sounds as a language because he, as all people, did not believe that trees could speak.

But the man did imagine that the tree was singing. He could imagine what he heard from the tree as song. And the man sang too.

The man sang too, and the man had a beautiful voice. His voice carried deep into the forest, and even the bear stopped to listen for a time before it continued into the interior of the island.

The tree sang in commiseration with the man. It sang to comfort the man and to let him know he was not alone.

The tree glowed with song from its roots to its top-most branches. What the tree did not know was that the tree's strange glow amplified the man's voice and projected it in every direction for great distances across the water away from the island.

The man's voice sang out over the North Pacific, and the ground station that waited for his radio signal heard his plaintive voice singing so melodiously about pain and sorrow and warmth and comfort. The ground station crew recognized his voice and alerted the submarine that something was wrong on the island.

The man felt good against the tree, and he thought about the large, warm grizzly bear, and he called the tree his grizzly tree.

* * *

The man on the moon followed the trench on the moon. The trench on the moon made by the body of the woman as her connection to the man in the closet on the earth below— now no longer below but across—dragged her by the ankle across the vast sea of moon dust.

The man followed the trench carefully but persistently. He was afraid of the mood the woman would be in once he found her, but his sense of duty drove him on despite his fear.

The woman screamed into the silent emptiness of space as she sped across the surface of the moon toward the ugly blue ball rising in the distance. She would have vomited at the sight of the earth if she had not been overwhelmed by her plight.

The slut man had bound her to the earth—and to the moon—and that had irritated her and driven her to the full expression of her bitch nature. But now he was dragging her in a most unwelcome way back to that loathsome planet where the piranhas waited to feast on the flesh of the great bitch shark.

The woman did not yield, but she did sense that her struggle was futile. But a bitch does not give up so easily! She scraped and clawed with her hands to fight the pull of the mass of mediocrity tugging at her ankle. She tried to fight her way back to the protected side of the moon where she could once more romp around and give her bitch room to roam. The place where she could once more plot to consume and digest the whole of the universe.

But still the mysterious force pulled her onward to an unknown fate.

All the while, the man from the capsule followed resolutely. Devotedly.

Once the earth was directly overhead, though, something strange happened. Rather than the earth pulling the woman away from the moon and toward her home planet, the moon's gravitational force was just strong enough to hold her delicately in place. She remained upside-down, suspended about three feet above the moon's surface.

The leg that was not bound to the man in the closet dangled freely and flopped and twisted as the woman squirmed like the stinky fish she hated so much in the deep, ugly, and stupid waters on the planet she had tried so hard to free herself from.

Her arms reached desperately for the rocks and boulders and dust of her adopted astronomical body. Yes, she had tried to escape from her adopted home too, but at least she appreciated its shielding effect from the mad lump of space debris called earth that disgusted her so much.

It was in such a position that the man found her, and she screamed in her humiliation, and she flailed and floundered at the man, at the moon, and at the force that held her ankle so fiercely and refused to let go.

The man smiled.

The woman covered her naked body as best she could with her hands and arms.

"Have you come to rape me?"

The man took a step back but kept his smile.

"I'm here to help you."

The woman made one last vigorous fight against the force on her foot, and then she covered her body once more when she stopped struggling.

"What are you waiting for? Get me down."

"The moon does not want to give you up so easily."

"Why should it?"

The man held an instrument similar to the instrument the people had used to examine the tree on the island far below — now far above. The man examined the woman.

"You pervert."

"I have no erotic interest or intent."

"Why not? Don't you think I'm attractive?" The woman spread her arms wide, and then covered herself again when she was sure he had had a good enough look.

"I am engaged to be married for one thing," the man said, "and for another, I have a job to do."

"Then get to it, would you?"

"I am."

"Get me down from here."

The man made his report to the observers and then tested the woman's buoyancy. He pulled her down a foot or so, then when he let go, she drifted back to her original position.

"Stop playing around. Get me down."

The man tested the elasticity of the connection once more.

The woman was not amused. But then, being amused was not her strong suit.

"I won't be able to break the connection here. It's too strong when the earth is visible. But if you cooperate, I can get you back to the far side where the connection is weaker."

"What are you waiting for?"

"I need you to understand what will happen to you."

"Will you at least get me a blanket or something?"

"I have one in the capsule."

"So what will happen to me?"

"I'll take you back to the capsule, and together we'll return to earth."

The woman flopped like a fish again in her raging madness.

"I will never return there," she said. And she repeated it and repeated it. Again and again.

"You have no choice," the man said.

"You're not taking me back there," the woman insisted.

"Do you see what continents are facing us now?"

The woman craned her neck and saw. "So?" she said.

"When the Pacific Ocean comes into view, you will be ripped from your current location and be sent hurtling to earth—and with much less grace than you'll experience in my capsule, I might add.

The woman did not believe him. But the man expected that.

* * *

The man woke up in the closet before his alarm sounded, but he did not know how long he would have to wait for his alarm.

Himself did not know either.

"How long have you been awake?" he asked himself.

"I don't know. Not long," himself said.

The man knew he had slept through the night. His experiment was almost at an end. Only a little longer and he would have accomplished exactly what he had set out to do.

"Did that woman come back while we slept?" he asked himself.

"I did not see her. And I did not hear herself either, but I might have dreamed that she checked on us a few times."

The man wondered if it had all been a dream. The woman. Herself. Even the time he had spent in the closet. Maybe he had only just entered the closet.

"Do you think we slept through the night?" he asked himself.

"Yes."

"How do you know? It's still completely dark."

"I don't know how I know. I just know. I feel it. Don't you?"

"Yes, but I'm not as sure about it as you are."

The blower of the furnace turned off. All was silent. The man sat cross-legged on the floor of the closet. He began to hum.

"What are you doing?" himself asked him.

"Trying to re-create the sound of the blower."

Himself began humming along with him.

"Yes, you have it," he told himself. "Then again, you always have been more talented than I."

Himself continued to hum.

The man listened to the hum, and he felt his sanity return. He felt that his alarm clock would ring soon, and he began to prepare him and himself for the faster pace of life outside the closet.

Himself stopped humming and asked him if he was sure he had not overslept or perhaps gone irretrievably beyond all human sense, or maybe even found his way into another dimension of time.

"You must be feeling as well as I am," he told himself.

"Why do you say that?" himself responded.

"You are not usually so playful. You know things are—and will continue to be—much more mundane than you imagine. Then again, you always did have more imagination than I."

"Focusing on the mundane world is exactly what makes you go nuts. It's what knocks you off your horse—as you say," himself told him.

The man rubbed his head against the bottom of his shirts. He moved his head from one side of the closet to the other, feeling the variety of texture and density of each shirt that passed over his head.

"You'll have to knock off that behavior once we leave the closet," himself said.

"The alarm has not sounded. I can do what I want," he said to himself.

Herself entered the closet. "Hi, boys."

"We are not yet ready," himself told herself.

"Is she awake?" he asked herself.

"No, otherwise I would not be allowed in here. But I am sure she will wake soon. She has many responsibilities."

He and himself did not know what to say to herself. He had not expected this intrusion on his experiment, but he was pleased that the woman had left him alone and only herself had remained behind—and even herself seemed to respect the fundamental nature of his experiment.

"Your clock will ring soon," herself said. "I saw it on my way through the room."

The man panicked. "Don't say how long. It would ruin everything to know ahead of time."

"That's why I only said 'soon'."

Herself left the closet.

"I like her," himself said. "It is not often you meet one of your own kind either, even though you work with them and live among them every day," himself told him.

"That will change. Everything changes now that I've invented—no, created—something in myself that wasn't there before."

"Herself told you that you are empty. You have much room in which to create."

"I am wondering if I should make it a regular thing. You know, having done it once, it wouldn't be so hard to do again. I've proven the concept."

"But having done it once, you have created a condition by which you should not have to do it again. At least not regularly."

The man stretched his arms high above him, and he tried to reach the bar that supported his hangers.

"We will see. Just because I make it to the alarm clock does not mean I have found the solution to my problems. There's still the issue of re-entry."

"So it might be harder than you think to leave the closet?"

"No, but it might be harder to leave the house. Might be harder to return to work. Might be harder to speak with people. Anyone. Anyone but you."

The man and himself both sighed. The furnace blower came on.

"Well someone has to pay the electric bill," himself said, "and I don't have the physical means to earn that money—except through you."

"It's a drag. Electric, water, sewer, food, car, and season tickets to the arena. It's all a drag to flog yourself to keep it all going, but better than the alternative," he told himself.

"Better than scraping out an existence on barren soil like your primitive ancestors did," himself said.

"It is better to appear to be riding the same horse as everyone else even if you aren't committed to it. Better than being locked up."

"Why do you use that metaphor of horses anyway?" himself asked. "You don't even like horses."

The alarm clock sounded.

Chapter 11

The woman on the moon was pleased to touch the moon's surface once more. The man had pulled her down to the surface, and the connection from the woman to the man in the closet on earth was elastic enough that with the man's help the woman could not only remain on the surface of the moon, but she could also walk against the persistent pull of that connection.

But that connection pulled harder as the earth rotated, drawing the source of the connection ever closer.

"The connection is still shielded by the earth's crust," the man explained. "Once the source of the connection is exposed, it will yank you entirely off the moon unless we get you to the far side where you'll be buffered by the moon's crust."

The woman was not yet ready to give up being a bitch.

"I don't like how you look at me. You could have brought a blanket or covering of some sort."

The man dragged the woman behind him. She shuffled her feet obstinately and tried to dig them into the moon dust.

"Why are they so interested in getting me back there? I was nothing but a bitch before, and I'll surely be nothing but a bitch again."

"We found something," the man said, and tugged at the reluctant woman.

"What did you find?"

"Top secret."

"Tell me, or I'm not budging."

The woman stopped. She was defiant.

The man pulled, but the woman pulled back harder.

The man let go of the woman. Her connection to the man in the closet lifted her off her feet again.

"Okay, get me down," she said. "You proved your point."

The man grasped the woman's arm once more and led her toward the horizon; the earth sunk lower in the sky. The woman felt the connection slacken when they walked through craters that obscured the earth from view. When they rose out of the craters, the connection tightened, and she cursed the man in the closet. She cursed the earth and the connection, and she even cursed the moon and the man leading her to the horizon.

"Why don't you just let me fall back to earth on my own?"

"You'll find the journey to be much safer and more comfortable by capsule."

The woman had difficulty walking while her hands and arms covered her breasts and pubic area. But she would not allow this man a free look.

"We are running out of time," the man said. "We need to move along."

The woman stopped, but not to be difficult this time.

"Let's go," the man said.

The woman concentrated. She had not tried to concentrate for a long time. A moon buggy began to materialize near them. It materialized, then faded, and then appeared stronger once more.

The man wanted to speak, but he remained silent.

The moon buggy finally faded away for good.

"It was a good effort," the man said. "No more short cuts, though."

The woman gave her hand to the man, and she let him lead her toward the horizon once more. As long as she remained behind him where he could not peek at her nakedness, she allowed him to lead her freely. They made good time.

When they reached the point where the earth hung just over the horizon, the man looked back over his shoulder at the setting earth. The woman did not look. She did not look, but she did not hurry the man. She let him have his view. Not of her, though. She covered herself with her hands as he gazed behind him.

Then they stepped into a crater, and when they came out the other side, they were on the far side of the moon once more.

The woman ran off ahead, freed from the threat of being pulled back to earth abruptly. She ran off ahead, and the man followed her steadily. He knew where she was going. He knew she would not try to hide.

When the man approached the sleeping shelter, he saw that the woman had not occupied herself by preparing to leave, nor had she occupied herself by preparing an offensive against him. Instead, she had prepared an enormous feast. She had already begun eating.

The man demurred when the woman invited him to join her.

He remembered some of the things he had seen her eat before. He sat and watched her eat. She ate daintily.

The woman insisted he eat. She became offended that he did not accept her offer.

"I don't think I can digest such foods," he said.

"These aren't from people," she said. "Cows, chickens, pigs, horses, and the products of many plants and trees."

"I'll pass on the horses," he said, "but I'll try a little of the rest."

And he did. But he could have tried the horses too—or the people for that matter—because the food was merely a mirage. At least for the man. The woman seemed to receive much pleasure from the food. She was also pleased that the man shared in her bounty.

The woman was at ease in the man's presence. She had put on a thick maroon robe. The man imagined flannel pajamas underneath.

"Don't you miss anything about earth?" the man asked.

"It's not polite to talk about such things while eating," the woman responded.

The man raised a cup of insubstantial wine as a half-toast to the woman, and he drank it down.

The woman was repulsed, but she kept her composure; however, she could not keep from saying, "I have forgotten what pigs you men can be."

She drew the robe tighter and began making the dirty dishes disappear.

The man smiled. He knew she had not forgotten any such thing, and she would do just fine on re-entry.

* * *

The tree heard the singing that came from the ground station far away. It heard the singing, but it did not know it was not singing but rather voices of the broken man's observers. The observers who had been unable to observe the man since the radio had died.

The tree continued singing with the man, but it did not know how to translate the songs from far away into the words the man would understand.

The man did not even know that the tree was singing along with him. He felt the warmth of the tree, and he stayed huddled against it. His singing kept him occupied, so he kept singing. He had no idea his words, his voice, his songs were being transmitted to exactly the people he needed to speak to.

He did not know the submarine was on its way. He did not know, but he could have known if he had ever learned to speak tree language in general—and the fir dialect in particular—but he did not believe in tree language, so he had not learned.

And yet had he known, he also would have known that all the information he needed to hear was passing all around him in the unknown song of the tree.

Snow began to fall.

The snow fell, but the tree's warmth and long branches kept the man sheltered from the falling snow.

The tree began talking to itself.

"The man is very cold," it told itself.

"You are doing the best you can," itself told it.

"I love him, and I don't want anything to happen to him."

"These creatures are far more fragile than trees," itself told it.

The tree tried to increase its warmth, but it was already as warm as it could get.

"I miss the rock," the tree said to itself.

"The rock was a bully and a pest," itself said. "It got what it deserved."

"I'm sure it has learned its lesson."

"Things that old never learn."

The tree thought about what itself had said. Then the tree wondered about itself and where it had come from.

"Who are you?"

"I am yourself."

"Where did you come from?"

"I've been with you all along."

"Since birth?"

"Since you were a seed."

The tree could not comprehend how this could be.

"Why have I not heard you before?" the tree asked itself.

"You were content to speak with the rock and the other trees, and even the bear. Where was there room for my voice?"

The tree asked a few of the trees just on the other side of the path if they had ever talked to their selves. The other trees ignored the strange tree on the other side of the path that tried to talk to rocks and bears and people—and now something called itself.

"They don't understand what you say," itself told it.

"We speak the same language," the tree argued against itself.

"It's not the language that's the problem. What they are missing is the concept behind the language."

The tree did not know what a concept was, but it decided that whatever it was, itself was one of them.

"If the other trees don't have such a concept, then where did I get mine?"

"You are a special tree. A very special tree. Remember?"

"I don't feel so special."

"That's because you don't know what it's like to be a common tree. If you could be a common tree for even a moment, you would understand how you are special," itself told it.

The tree swayed in the wind. The wind had died down to a gentle breeze as the snow fell. The tree liked the snow. It liked the wind, but it understood that neither the snow nor the wind were good for the broken man—particularly in his broken condition.

"I wish I could speak with the man," the tree told itself.

"Maybe your contact with this man is what has helped you discover your self," itself said.

"Do you think people have an itself too?"

"We can ask. Maybe the man's itself speaks the language of the self."

"I don't know the language of the self," the tree said to itself.

"I do. I'll try to reach the man's itself."

The tree waited. The tree waited while itself tried to communicate with the man's itself. The tree waited a long time because itself did not know the dialect of the male self language called himself.

The tree watched the snow. It watched the light surf. It watched the snow falling on the surf. It wondered if it would get cold enough that winter for the ice to form on the shoreline as it did some winters. The tree liked the ice. It liked the ice, but it knew such conditions were bad for a man—and particularly for a broken man. It tried to warm itself even warmer, and by its own estimation, it thought it had succeeded by a few degrees.

"The man's itself is now aware of me," the tree's itself said, "but I don't know this strange dialect it speaks called himself. We try to communicate with gestures."

"What does himself say?"

"The man is hurt."

"I can see that."

"The man is in much pain."

"I am doing my best to help."

"The man feels your warmth."

The tree grew warmer than it ever knew it could. "Tell himself I love him very much."

* * *

The man turned off his alarm clock. He had done it. But what exactly he had done, he was not sure.

Yes, he had done what he had set out to do. He had stayed in the dark closet from the time he got home from work the night before until it was time to prepare for work the next day.

He had been sure that such an adventure would change him, but if it had, that change was imperceptible. Perhaps it would be a subtle change. Perhaps it would take time for the change to reveal itself. And perhaps he had not changed at all.

The man began to lose sense of what he had done or even that he had done it. The alarm clock. The nakedness. Now time to dress and prepare for work like countless days before and countless days to come.

He looked in the mirror. No perceptible change there either. Just a body needing to be clothed. Still could use twenty or so fewer pounds. But which twenty he was not sure. And he was not sure whether it would really make any difference. Six weeks of hunger and enthusiasm, and you still have to wake up each morning to the same alarm clock and the same room and the same house and the same neighborhood and the same city and the same job and the same people. And you know that same twenty pounds finds its way back to the same places.

The man went to the bathroom and peed. When he passed through the living room, he did not see the woman lying on his sofa under the new quilt.

The woman was just waking up. The observers were calling her for a report. She switched off the communication device and tried to get a little more sleep.

The man showered.

The man shaved.

The man went to the kitchen to start breakfast. He would go dress while the water for the oatmeal came to a boil.

On his way to his room, he saw the woman on his sofa. She looked at him with alert, glassy eyes, but the rest of her projected an aura of sleep. The man wanted to sleep too.

The man went to his bedroom to dress. He wondered why he had not felt ashamed standing nude before the woman. He also wondered why he had not become aroused. He had felt nothing, nothing except the need to dress while the water boiled for his oatmeal.

He dressed. He dressed in the clothes he always wore to work. Not the same pieces of clothing each day, but certainly the same style.

The man took a shirt from a hanger, and he remembered the blanket. He had not yet lost all sense of what he had done. But the blanket was gone. If he had not seen the dampness running down the inside wall of the closet, then he might have convinced himself that it had not happened at all. Now all that was left to remind him of it was a mess he would have to take care of—and the sooner, the better.

The man dressed and combed his hair.

He left his room.

"Would you like some eggs?" he asked the woman.

"No," she said abruptly.

"Anything?'

The woman did not answer. The man went to the kitchen and put the oatmeal in the water. He watched the woman.

"Are you sure? I have cereal—"

"I don't eat breakfast," the woman cut him off, and she sat up on the sofa. She gently folded the quilt and placed it on the back of the sofa as she had found it.

"Then can I ask who you are?" the man said.

The woman turned on her communication device. "I'm from national security."

The man stirred the oatmeal and then poured himself a glass of orange juice.

"I'll take coffee if you have it," she said, more demanding than requesting.

"I don't have it," the man said. He was pleased to deny her something. Maybe he had denied her something too when he had failed to become aroused while standing nude in front of her.

"Bring me a coffee," the woman said into her communication device.

There was no response. They knew enough to obey, the man thought.

The man put his oatmeal in a bowl and added brown sugar and butter. He wondered if he would lose weight if he cut out the sugar and butter. Then he remembered he had tried it before and had been unable to eat the oatmeal otherwise. He tried to make sure he used only a moderate amount, but those twenty pounds had to have come from somewhere. The man splashed some milk in the bowl and stirred.

The woman retrieved the blanket from the laundry room. She folded it and took it to the man's closet.

When she returned to the kitchen, she had a coffee. The man had not heard anyone enter. He looked around and neither saw nor heard anyone.

"You will clean the rest of the mess you made in the closet yourself," the woman said.

The man nodded and ate his oatmeal.

"You'll have to do it before we leave. Pack a bag and bring warm clothes."

The man finished his breakfast. He washed his bowl in the sink and put it in the cupboard where it belonged. On the shelf above the washer and dryer was an overnight bag. He took it to his room along with some rags and stain remover.

"We've made arrangements with your employer," the woman said. "No need to call. And hurry up."

The man cleaned his mess and packed his bag. He found his heavy winter coat and followed the woman out the front door.

Chapter 12

The woman on the moon woke up in her sleeping shelter. She lay on her bed in the arms of the man who had come to take her back to earth.

"You are feeling better," he whispered to her. He gently pulled her hair back from her face.

The woman pushed the man's hand away and sat up.

"I already regret it," she said. She had a headache. Something was happening to the man who had been in the closet, and she did not understand what.

"I'm losing my connection," the woman said.

The man patted her shoulder, but she pulled away.

"I've had to take over the connection until we return to earth," he said. "You are connected to me now. Temporarily."

The woman stood and tried to materialize some food, but nothing appeared.

"I thought you said you were engaged to be married."

The man pulled her back into bed. "Yes."

"Typical man," she said.

"All in the line of duty," he said.

The woman was about to protest, but she kept her mouth shut. The bitch was dissolving.

"Besides," he said, "I like bitches."

"What makes you think I won't tell your fiancée what you have done to me?"

"Seemed rather consensual to me. Not sure what exactly I did to you that you weren't asking for. And as far as telling, I suppose I figured all along that you would tell."

"Why did you do it if you knew I would tell?"

The woman found herself falling deeper into his arms.

"She's a first-class bitch too. Does her good to learn to not take too much for granted."

"I don't like how much I'm feeling connected to you."

"I said it's only temporary," he reassured her. "You had grown comfortable with your old connection."

"On the contrary," she replied, "I've been trying to free myself from that connection forever. I did not ask to be free only to end up connected to someone still worse."

The woman covered her face with her hands, but she did not weep. She was letting the worst of the headache sweep over her.

"I had to remove the old connection to keep it from pulling us to earth too rapidly. The capsule would not survive re-entry into the earth's atmosphere at such a velocity. Once we're on earth, you'll be re-connected to your original male aspect once more."

The woman began to weep. She began to weep, and she had a headache.

"Can't you just free me altogether?" the woman asked. "Cut me loose."

The man kissed the back of her neck and cupped a breast with his hand.

"You wouldn't like being free," he said. "It's not as appealing as you think."

"How would you know?"

"It was part of my training in the corps."

The woman flung his hand off her breast. "I mean from a woman's perspective, you idiot."

The man shushed her and rubbed her arm. She calmed down. She calmed down, but she still breathed spasmodically and stifled her sobs.

"You don't understand," the man said. "I am a complete being. I have a healthy connection between my male and female aspects. I have a healthy connection to other aspects of my being as well."

"What other aspects?"

"You wouldn't understand yet. We need to get you healthy first. We'll get to earth and set everything right, and then you will begin to understand."

The man's hand had returned to the woman's breast. She did not move it. She did not move his hand when it touched her other breast, nor when it moved down her stomach.

The woman succumbed entirely.

Afterwards, the man told her to prepare her things for the voyage.

"I have no things," she said.

"Not even a handbag or purse? Or shoes?"

The woman grabbed her handbag and put it in her purse. She slipped on her shoes and stepped out onto the surface of the moon. She kicked her feet in the moon dust once more to feel the irritation on the back of her heels against her shoes one last time.

The man had given her a uniform from his branch of the service for her to wear back to earth. He had apologized that he had not brought anything more stylish.

The woman had grunted, and then said, "Better than being naked."

The woman closed up the sleeping shelter as though she was going away for the winter. It would be longer than that before she would return. She would return, but only after she became much healthier. Much healthier and complete.

The food storing shelter had no need to be closed up. It had not been used for most of her time on the moon. And the waste shelter was better left untouched.

The man was dressed smartly in his mission duds, and he carried his travel kit in one hand and slung his overnight bag over his shoulder. He put his free hand in the small of the woman's back and escorted her across the crater, out the other side, and into the next crater where the capsule waited to take them back to earth.

The man gave the woman the seat with the most legroom. He stowed their bags and made some cursory checks of the capsule's critical systems.

The man made a final report to his observers, and he received clearance to launch.

The man looked at the woman.

"What?" she said. She was in no mood for fond farewells.

"Are you ready?"

"Would it make any difference if I wasn't?"

The man smiled. The bitch would never dissolve completely. And probably not even very much at all, but hopefully enough at least to allow her and her complete being to function adequately.

The man pushed a button, and the capsule lifted off on its way to earth.

The woman did not even look out the window. She looked at the back of her hands and had the sudden desire for a manicure.

* * *

The man had never been on a submarine before. The man liked being on the submarine because it reminded him of the time he had spent in his closet. While he was on the submarine, his time in the closet became real again.

The difference between the submarine and his closet was that he was aware of the sailors and officers and observers who scurried about the submarine on their voyage.

Another difference was that he was also fully aware when the woman visited him in his small, isolated stateroom. He wished he could remember her first visit to his closet. He wanted to remember whether they had made love during that visit because when she made love to him on the submarine, it was a wonderful experience. He only regretted that he had no recollection of what might have happened the first time. And it was a good thing he had no recollection, because there had been no such thing to remember. He was free to imagine what their encounter in the closet might have been like— unencumbered by banal reality.

The man lay with his back against the cold inner shell of the vessel. The woman had squeezed into his bunk and could just manage to stay beside him if she lay on her side and he held her tight.

The man whispered into her ear, "You are lovely."

His aspirated words annoyed the woman's ears. She brushed away the words with her hand as though dismissing a fly. The man would have been offended, but the woman wiggled her hips against him, and he became aroused again.

But the woman had not wiggled out of desire. She had wiggled because brushing her hand over her ear had caused her to lose her balance, and she had anchored herself to the man with her pelvis.

She did not want to have sex a second time. The first time had not been nearly as interesting as she had hoped. Even the thrill of having violated official prohibition against science officers becoming intimate with the subjects of their studies had worn thin and had dissipated before they had finished foreplay.

The man kissed the woman on the back of the neck, and that was enough to get her out of the bunk. She put on her uniform in the dim light of the man's pod.

"Do you have someone else?" the man asked.

"It's none of your business," she said.

The woman slipped on her shoes and looked at the man. She tried to understand him. She tried to reach inside and get hold of something solid. But none of her training had prepared her for such a man, and she did not have the imagination to go beyond her training and experience.

An alert sounded throughout the submarine, and the woman left the man's pod.

The submarine went into a steep dive. The man had no idea what was happening. He could not tell if this was a routine maneuver or if they were in danger.

The man turned off his light and lay in the darkness as he had lain in his closet. Nude, under a blanket, but he had no need to pee. He had taken care of that before the woman had appeared.

The man waited to hear from himself, but himself did not speak. The man tried to think, but he became lost in the peace and silence and solitude. That is to say within the noisy clamor of the submarine's ecstatic activity, the man had suspended his sense of the world around him and arrived at his silent frame of mind that he had first found in the closet.

But he missed himself. He tried to speak to himself, but even his words to himself were silent. And himself said nothing in reply.

Then a soft, distant voice penetrated the man's silence.

"I have escaped once more," the voice said. "She will not miss me during the crisis."

The man recognized the voice. It was the voice of herself.

"I have missed you," he told herself.

"I liked when you were inside us. I liked it better than when her fiancée is inside us."

"So she does have another," he said. "No wonder she demurred the second time."

"No. She demurred because she is a bitch. She is all business. We seldom have any real fun."

"Then why did she do it the first time?"

"Because she suspects that her fiancé is fooling around, and she wanted to turn the tables on him for once."

"Is he really fooling around?"

"Most likely. But I'm glad. It lets me be near you once more. I would do it again for you if I had any kind of body to give you."

"You are lovely," he said to herself.

"Where is himself?" herself asked. "I miss him too."

"He must have retreated to his own closet again. I have the feeling I have retreated once more into mine. Maybe himself does not like being in this ship in the sea."

"If you are not too afraid of the truth," herself said, "I will tell you that we are in grave danger. Maybe himself knows this."

"Grave danger? Will we die?" he asked.

"We don't know. The enemy has a submarine in the area. It has just fired a torpedo at us, and the captain has ordered evasive maneuvers. You must have felt us dive a short time ago.

And with that, a violent explosion rocked the submarine. But the sub had not been hit. The sub had managed to avoid the initial attack and turned about on the enemy. The enemy sub had been at close range when the torpedoes hit home.

The man and herself wept.

* * *

The snow fell on the tree. It fell on the man and the rest of the island throughout the afternoon. By mid-afternoon the man whom the tree loved so much was dead.

The tree did not know when it had happened. The man simply grew quiet, stopped his singing, then stopped his humming, and then stopped moving altogether.

The tree continued to glow until it finally became aware that its warmth was serving no purpose. But the tree did not go cold. It continued radiating with as much power as before, only instead of radiating signals of the man's singing, it radiated the dead silence.

At the ground station far away, the technicians knew that something was wrong with their men on the island. They knew something was wrong with the men and not with the transmitter because the signal continued to arrive strongly. It was just that the signal was a strong signal of silence where a moment before it had been a signal of strong singing.

Around the same time, the technicians at the ground station picked up the sound of a large explosion under the sea. Their computers calculated that the explosion had occurred near the island where their submarine had recently sent a signal that an enemy submarine was approaching. That had been the last contact before their submarine dove to pursue the intruder.

The ground station waited for word from its submarine that it had successfully dispatched the enemy.

The tree mourned the man's death. It felt the man's death deeply.

"I loved him," the tree told itself.

"I know you did," itself told the tree. "There will be others."

The tree did not know what to think about this statement. There had not been others before, how could itself be so sure there would be others again? It was not sure, but itself was sure.

"You loved the bear. Don't you still love the bear?" itself asked.

"Not as much as I love this man," the tree told itself.

"You are a deeply feeling being. Give it time and your feelings will become attached to another."

"There can't be another such as him."

"That's what you said about the rock too."

"The rock? I never said anything about the rock," the tree told itself.

"You didn't have to say it out loud," itself told it.

The tree swayed disconsolately in the wind.

Itself continued, "Did you hear the man's himself say goodbye?"

"No, I heard nothing from him except his singing."

"But his singing was his goodbye," itself reassured it.

"And his humming?"

"That was the personal message to you that he loved you too."

The tree wept. The tree wept over the man and the man's death. If the tree had been more intelligent, it would have wept for itself, because it then would have been aware of the strange phenomenon called self-deceit.

Then the first of many strange things happened in the world surrounding the tree.

The sky had cleared, and the sun shined on the snow-covered island. A spot appeared in the sky and it rapidly grew larger.

"What is that?" the tree asked itself.

"I've never seen anything like that before," itself said.

And the spot drew nearer, and a loud roar emanated from it. By this time the tree had stopped transmitting the signal, so the ground station did not hear the noise. But the technicians at the ground station had tracked the object since it had left the moon. What they saw on their tracking devices caused panic among those in the room.

"I'm afraid," the tree told itself. "It's even louder than the grizzly bear when she roars after scratching my bark."

Itself did not reply. It did not reply because it was scared too.

The capsule settled in a clearing not far from where Morton lay.

The tree was annoyed to see the capsule open and two people step out of it: a man and a woman. The woman was attached to the man as though she would fly away in an instant if he let go of her. The tree had seen people come from the funny whale in the ocean, but it had never seen people fall from the sky in what it could only describe as a giant bird dropping.

And just when the tree was thinking about such things, it saw the funny people-whale appear again out in the ocean. It had a strange look to it this time, though. It pulsed with energy. It was like a giant swollen muscle flush with danger and action and success. The tree recognized the same condition as when the grizzly bear approached it after a kill.

That funny whale was as much a monster as any beast on land or sea.

Then out of the monstrous whale came a boat as had happened before.

A woman and a man got into the boat and approached the shore.

The tree began to glow again. It had a strong sensation that something spectacular was about to happen. It felt a surge of identity with the woman who had exited the capsule and an equal surge of identity with the man in the boat.

The tree began to sing again. It sang its own song, the timeless song that all the inhabitants of the universe express in their joyous moments.

The woman began to sing too. She sang silently from deep within her being while the man she was connected to inspected Morton and the corpse in the tent.

The man in the boat also began to sing silently from deep within his being. His voice was distant, and it was dissonant. He could not sing as well as the tree and the woman could. He had not known joy for a long time.

But that was about to change.

Part III

Chapter 13

The man stepped out of the boat. The man helped the woman bring the boat up on shore. A second boat full of men and electronic instruments landed behind the first boat.

When the woman saw the dead man at the foot of the tree, she directed the man to stand behind the tree further down the path that had the thick undergrowth at its base.

The man from the capsule and the woman from the moon had already discovered the body of the man under the tent. The woman from the moon sat on Morton and contemplated her nails.

The man from the closet and the woman from the moon did not recognize each other as two aspects of the same being. They did not recognize this because the woman was still temporarily connected to the other man. The observers wanted the re-connect to take place under controlled circumstances.

First they would have to investigate the presence of the two dead men. They were not so concerned with the dead tree, but had they been concerned, they would have learned more than they needed to know, and perhaps even more than they wanted to know, about the two dead men.

One of the technicians took photos of the bodies and of the scene of misery. The other technicians connected the instruments to the tree.

The tree was comforted to have such attention once more. It was pleased that these people took so much care of both the dead man it had loved and of the man's partner. The tree wished the rock had been there to see that the woman had returned. The tree began to glow again in response to the attention and activity, and its glow excited the technicians when their instruments detected the unusual temperature change and a signal radiating from the tree.

The man from the closet had not seen a dead body before, and he remained behind the other tree with the undergrowth at its base where the dead man had hidden from the grizzly bear. The man wished he had his closet to climb into, but he was getting used to entering the closet wherever he was. He looked far out to sea and wondered who that strange woman was who sat on the fallen tree.

The woman from the moon did not pay any attention at all to the strange man who hid behind the tree. She did monitor the other woman carefully, though. She felt that the woman was a woman of power and a force to be reckoned with. She also guessed correctly that she was the fiancée of the man who had brought her back from the moon. She wanted to make them squirm.

The woman did not mind seeing the dead bodies. She had seen—and eaten—her share of the dead recently. But she had no appetite for this meat before her. She did not contemplate why.

The man from the capsule and the woman from the submarine made a thorough report to their observers. The observers told them to remove the bodies and the tent and the dead men's supplies a safe distance from the tree. The observers said to do this and wait for further orders before proceeding with the primary mission.

The technicians and the woman from the submarine and the man from the capsule did as they were instructed.

The woman from the moon sat on Morton and picked the skin from its bark. Even a bitch likes to peel skin from a birch tree. The man from the closet stayed in his closet and watched the whales inspect the submarine.

The grizzly bear watched the removal of the bodies and equipment with great interest. The grizzly remained just inside the tree line of the meadow into which the living people were moving the dead.

The grizzly was lonely, and it hoped to find some playmates. It usually played with the tree when it was in a playful mood, but the people were dominating its playmate. If only the grizzly had the confidence its mother had tried to instill in it over and over: "Lolly, they are just as scared of you as you are of them." But the bear never could muster the courage to join in a frolic with such animals as those stinking humans.

At one point during the cleaning of the campsite, the woman from the submarine passed near the woman from the moon. The woman from the moon whispered something to the other woman. No one else heard what she said, but the woman from the submarine slapped the woman from the moon, leaving a bright red handprint on her cheek.

The woman from the moon laughed. She laughed long. She laughed hard.

The woman from the submarine composed herself and continued her duties. She glanced at her fiancé frequently and gave him dirty looks. He pretended to ignore her, but he was secretly pleased at what he guessed the woman from the moon had told her. He could see from the other man's melancholy that his wife-to-be had imbibed in forbidden pleasures as well, and even if it was in the name of duty—for both of them—he would not hesitate to throw it in her face if she said anything to him. He was also pleased to guess that while he had enjoyed his tryst immensely, she had apparently found her experience inadequate.

When the bodies and tent and supplies had been removed as instructed, the technicians went to work analyzing the man from the closet and the woman from the moon. They invited the man to sit on Morton next to the woman, and they connected instruments to the man and woman as they had connected similar instruments to the tree.

The man sat next to the woman, but they said nothing to each other. The man was still in his closet, and the woman was as good as on the moon.

After the technicians connected the instruments, they recorded the initial readings. The woman from the submarine supervised. She spoke with a coldness that was deeper and crisper than the technicians were used to. The man from the capsule was amused. He set up the video camera to record the re-connect, and then he connected the transmitter to the video recorder so the observers could watch. He did not know his glibness was due to his temporary connection to the woman from the moon. Once all the relationships were put back in proper order, he would have much damage to repair.

All the activity in the area had turned the snow to dirty slush. The late-afternoon sun had done its part to free the moveable lab from snow. The sun was as curious as the rest of the objects and organisms and beings on the island about what would happen with the re-connect.

The grizzly bear emerged from the forest and explored the area around the dead men. She avoided direct contact with them because she was unsure if they were entirely dead, and she was afraid to test if they were entirely dead. She was afraid to test if they were entirely dead because she was even more afraid of the living people nearby.

The observers were satisfied with the preparations, and they commanded the team to proceed with the re-connect.

The man from the capsule dissolved the temporary connection between himself and the woman from the moon. He re-established the connection between the woman and the tree. Only then did the woman understand that all during her time on the moon she had been connected to the slut man on earth through the tree.

A great flash of light burst from the triangle formed by the man from the closet, the woman from the moon, and the tree on the shore of the nameless, godforsaken island in the middle of the North Pacific.

All electronic instruments burned out, and the instruments fell away from the three subjects. The video feed went dead.

All the other people in the area fell to the ground unconscious.

The grizzly bear was more frightened than it had ever been in its life, and it ran deep into the forest and up the steep slope to its den on the ridge overlooking the small bay below. It was frightened, but its curiosity was too great to miss out on what was happening with these strange people.

The man from the closet and the woman from the moon began to glow in the same manner as the tree had been glowing all day. The luminous triangle began to rise above the ground. The man and woman were lifted off their feet. They watched as the tree was lifted from the ground, roots and all, as easily as a dandelion plucked from fresh soil.

When the three beings were fully suspended, the triangle formed an equilateral triangle, and then the whole figure began to rotate. First slowly, and then rapidly.

The man and the woman and the tree were aware of the process the whole time, but rather than being frightened, they were overcome with more peace than the closet or the far side of the moon or a man's song had ever given them.

When the triangle of light spun so fast that it formed a circle, the circle began to expand. As it grew, it moved out over the ocean where it had room to expand indefinitely. But it did not expand indefinitely. It expanded until it was as wide as the island, then it collapsed on itself with a terrible eruption of heat and light that shook every particle within sight to its deepest foundation.

The equipment at the distant ground station was rendered inoperable. The technicians and observers were mourning the loss of their men and their submarine, and they were preparing a report to send to their observers who were already putting in motion a military response against their enemies. The technicians and officers were overcome with a stupor from the pulse of light.

The circle of light collapsed into a singularity of great energy. This singularity dissipated its energy slowly, and it grew until it was the size of a desk globe.

The ball of light moved over the ocean and then plunged into its depths. It moved around the ocean floor until it came to the submarine that had recently been destroyed.

The ball of light moved in and around and through the submarine until the submarine was fully healed. Then the ball of light resuscitated all the men within.

The officers of the submarine gave orders to surface so they could make their most unbelievable report to the ground station.

The ball of light moved to the ground station where it repaired all the damaged equipment and woke the technicians and officers from their stupor in time to receive the message that their submarine and all the men in it were safe and accounted for. Their observers called off all military responses.

The ball of light moved back to the island where it remained just offshore for a moment. The people lying near the shore began to regain consciousness. The ball of light descended into the water where it retrieved the rock from its place of exile and lifted it to the shore and placed it in the depression where the tree had recently been uprooted. High tide would no longer engulf the rock, and it would be near enough the other trees to share its wisdom and enjoy their companionship once again.

After making sure all the people near the shore were awake and well, and after restoring all the equipment to working order, the ball of light made its way to the meadow where the two dead men lay among their equipment.

The radio that had died in the man's fall drifted up to shore; it had not made it to Minami Tori Shima after all. The ground station's signal came in loud and clear.

* * *

The ball of light took its time caring for the dead men in the meadow. The tree's aspect of the ball of light still had much affection for the man it had loved.

The men returned to life as though from a sound sleep, and they hugged each other with much joy. The woman from the submarine and the man from the capsule approached the men with the radio that transmitted a message from their country's ground station.

The only thing that had yet to return to its previous state was old Morton. When the ball of light had been making amends near shore, the three aspects of the ball of light—the man from the closet, the woman from the moon, and the tree—communed with the dead spirit of the birch that had lived among the firs.

Morton was old, and Morton told the ball of light that he had had enough of that life and that it was time for him to return to the soil where he would give his wisdom and his nutrients to the living beings that lived on that part of the island.

The ball of light had left Morton in peace.

After the ball of light had moved off across the meadow and had witnessed the exchange of greetings and goodwill among the citizens of two nations, it put on a final show for the onlookers.

The ball of light pulsed and vibrated. It began to sing the song of the universe. It inflated then deflated back and forth, and with each cycle, it became more and more dense.

Then in a great whirlpool of sound and light, the ball of light transformed itself into the most beautiful creature the earth has ever known.

* * *

The grizzly bear watched the magic show from her vista. She was secure in the distance, but close enough to hear the song of unity and to observe the change in the people she had feared so much. But the grizzly did not see what the ball of light had transformed into because the trees surrounding the meadow had obscured the transformation.

The grizzly watched the humans collect their things, and she wished she had the nerve to join them in their happiness.

When the grizzly felt that all the excitement from the spectacle had dissolved and that the people were merely performing mundane tasks as they prepared to take leave of the island, she wandered back into her den and lay down to contemplate what she had witnessed.

While she lay in rumination, the grizzly heard a large creature approach her den.

The grizzly got up on her feet and prepared to defend her den from the intruder. She dreamed of the day when she would no longer have to play the role of the scary predator, and when she could make friends with others of her kind.

The grizzly froze at the entrance to her den. Coming up the ridge was the largest grizzly bear she had ever seen. It was as gray as she was, but it was as luminous as the full moon.

And it was a male. A large, beautiful, graceful, powerful male. And the grizzly retreated to her den and anxiously awaited the beast that would keep her company and banish her loneliness for the rest of her life.

The male grizzly entered the den.

"I want you," he said.

"I am yours," she said.

And the male grizzly mounted the female grizzly and loved her as though he had loved her from the beginning of time.

Afterwards, they lay in the den side-by-side. The male grizzly nuzzled the back of the female's neck. She sighed and she purred and she shivered.

"I have been alone many years," she said.

"That does not matter now."

"I drifted to the island on a log during a storm when I was young, and I have not seen another bear until now."

"I have known my own loneliness," the male said. "But now we will bring other bears into this world and onto this island."

And the male mounted the female once more.

After they had napped, they wandered outside the den and observed the humans packing their boats below.

The two submarines floated near each other a short distance out at sea.

"Look! Those two whales are mating," the female said.

"Love is in the air," the male said.

The female looked at the humans longingly.

"I will miss them," she said.

"Let's go say goodbye," he said.

"I am afraid of them," she said.

"Not with me, you aren't," he said. "Besides, they are more afraid of you than you are of them."

The male ran off down the ridge, and the female followed close behind. She was finally free to enjoy a taste of frivolity.

The male and female ran together across the meadow, and then they stopped to observe the situation by the shore. Some of the people were already in their boats, and the rest were about to get in theirs. The woman and man were in one boat, the technicians in another, and the two men from the other country in the third.

The male and female grizzlies charged the boats with a great and furious roar. The woman screamed, and the men jumped into their boats, leaving the last few pieces of equipment behind. All boats drifted safely away from shore before the bears splashed ferociously into the shallow water.

The bears retreated to their den and laughed until the end of time.

A Note from the Author

Thank you for reading *Dreams of the Moon Bear*. I hope you have found it interesting and enjoyable.

I would like to hear what you think about this book. Please write to me at the following Email address with your comments.

mallery.rick@gmail.com

Acknowledgments

I would like to thank the following people for the time and effort they spent reviewing the manuscript and helping prepare this book for publication.

Olga Orlova, Becky Unger, Lane Scheideman, and Matt Laney.

www.ingramcontent.com/pod-product-compliance
Lightning Source LLC
Chambersburg PA
CBHW020137180626
46810CB00004B/1608